THE
PRODUCTIVITY
REVOLUTION
Control Your **Time** and
Get Things Done

MARC REKLAU

D1726423

RUPA

Published by
Rupa Publications India Pvt. Ltd 2019
7/16, Ansari Road, Daryaganj
New Delhi 110002

Sales Centres:
Allahabad Bengaluru Chennai
Hyderabad Jaipur Kathmandu
Kolkata Mumbai

Copyright © Marc Reklau 2019
This English language edition for Indian subcontinent published by
special arrangement with Montse Cortazar Literary Agency
(www.montsecortazar.com)

ISBN: 978-93-5333-612-7

First impression 2019

10 9 8 7 6 5 4 3 2 1

The moral right of the author has been asserted.

Printed at Nutech Print Services, Faridabad

THE
PRODUCTIVITY
REVOLUTION

Marc Reklau is a coach, speaker and a bestselling author. Marc's mission is to empower people to create the life they want and to give them the resources and tools to make it happen.

His message is simple: Many people want to change things in their lives, but few are willing to do a simple set of exercises constantly over a period of time. You can plan and create success and happiness in your life by installing habits that support you on the way to your goals.

If you want to work with Marc, directly contact him on his homepage www.marcreklau.com, where you can also find more information about him.

You can connect with him on Twitter @MarcReklau, Facebook or on his website www.goodhabitsacademy.com.

Disclaimer

This book is designed to provide information and motivation to our readers. It is sold with the understanding that the publisher is not engaged to render any type of psychological, legal or any other kind of professional advice. The instructions and advice in this book are not intended as a substitute for counseling. The content of each chapter is the sole expression and opinion of its author. No warranties or guarantees are expressed or implied by the author's and publisher's choice to include any of the content in this volume. Neither the publisher nor the individual author shall be liable for any physical, psychological, emotional, financial or commercial damages, including, but not limited to, special, incidental, consequential or other damages. Our views and rights are the same:

You must test everything for yourself according to your own situation, talents and aspirations.

You are responsible for your own decisions, choices, actions and results.

Contents

III: THE INNER GAME OF PRODUCTIVITY

IV: RECAP

Introduction

We say that time is the most precious thing we have and yet we waste it as if we are going to live forever. When you ask people why they don't go after their dreams or why they don't do more of what they love to do, the usual answers are: "I don't have enough money" or "I don't have enough time". Rich people usually answer with "I don't have enough time".With my friends and coaching clients, the most common excuse I hear almost all the time is "I don't have time", and even people who obviously have all the time in the world insist that they still never have enough.

I heard this so often in the last year after finishing my first two books that here I am, finally writing about time management and productivity—with the hope and desire that you can finally find the time for yourself that you need and want, to get things done and have more time to do the things you love. You can be a successful business person, entrepreneur, or employee *and* have enough time to spend with your family. The time is out there. So let's go and find it.

"Ok Marc. That's nice…but what's the revolution here?" you might ask.

The revolution is that we will not only have a look at the usual time management tools as listed in countless time management books over the years, but also at the "inner game of productivity" which examines you, your attitude, your beliefs etc. and—and here's the real revolution—we will look at exercises that make you happier!

It has been proven that happier brains are more productive brains. So if you are happy you will perform another 20 to 30% better with the same tools than a person in a neutral or pessimistic state. Now that's news, isn't it?

I'm still using the term "time management", because we've been using it forever, although by now we know that time can't be managed. We can only manage how we spend the time we have, which is—unless you can bend time—24 hours a day like every other person on this planet. And of course we are not managing time, but our priorities. I'm still going to use the term "time management", because I like it.

Some concepts might be repeated in the book. I didn't do that to be obnoxious or to stuff the book with unnecessary words. It is done because many concepts are interconnected and—okay, I admit—I also hope that by repetition the most important concepts stick better.

I also used less exclamation marks. A couple of readers complained about the huge numbers of exclamation marks in *30 Days—Change Your Habits, Change Your Life: A Couple of Simple Steps Every Day to Create the Life You Want*

… See, I'm taking your feedback seriously.

So why productivity? Easy. The more productive you are the more time you will have. Sounds boring? What about…the more productive you are the more money you will earn…either in your job, or starting a business on the side, or even earning money through a hobby of yours? Do I have your attention now? I do hope so!

As always, I only write about habits that I adopt in *my* life to get things done and move ahead. Those habits helped me to write two more books, design various online programs and workshops in the last 12 months, survive in my former job in a book printing company (probably the most efficient one in Europe—with only eight people taking care of over 1200 book projects a year), cut my working hours in half, and allowed me to never have to work a weekend or spend extra time at work.

It's funny. My friends say "Oh Marc, now that you are a bestselling author we probably have to ask for an appointment to see you." And yet I'm the one who always has time to see them and ends up asking them for an appointment…

Heck, I'm so productive, I don't even have an assistant, and still answer every single email myself—which, by the way, is a joy.

I know it's "in" to have a virtual assistant and play the "I'm-so-busy-and-have-so-many-clients-I-can't-even-answer-my-own-mails" card, but when I read that personal development guru Brendon Burchard did everything himself until he had his first million in his bank account, I decided that I can also get my stuff done myself. I also noticed that the most successful people answer their own emails because they are mostly also the most productive.

Back to productivity…

Productivity at work is a process that we usually ignore. We don't actually analyze our personal work processes and—at best—just try to get things done and have the least possible fires to put out along the way. And that, exactly, is the mistake.

When we become aware of our work processes we can start analyzing them and seeing where we lose this precious time, make corrections, and finally have all the time we need to get things done, and more.

Another problem is that people often don't see that there is a huge difference between **being busy** and **being productive**. We grew up in a culture where it was encouraged to be busy and work overtime and where being productive and organized was oftentimes seen as "not having a lot of work to do". And I'm not even talking about leaving work early or on time. You can be incredibly busy the whole day and not get any important work done.

But once you start going for results instead of being busy, things will change and it will make a huge difference.

My clients usually don't find blocks of time of 30 minutes or an hour. They find a minute here and three minutes there but it adds up.

The tools and habits that you will learn in this book are not new and there are no new secrets revealed. You probably know most of them. But that's the point. **Knowing is not enough**.

If you are tired of not having the time to do what you want and being busy all the time **you have to start taking action** and use some of the tools to find time.

Not all the tools work for everyone all the time.

Choose the ones you feel most comfortable with and start from there. Do them **consistently** over a period of time and analyze your results.

Most of what you will learn is common sense. But then again, **common sense is not common action,** or as others say, **"Common sense is the least common of all senses**."

This stuff works, but only if you do! It's simple, but not easy. If it was easy we'd all have enough time in our lives…and most of us don't. It's time to change that and I will once again revert to **habits**.

As Aristotle already knew nearly 2500 years ago, "We are what we repeatedly do. Excellence, then, is not an act, but a habit," and so is productivity.

If you are working overtime all the time and don't get your work done, then maybe it's time to change something, or as Albert Einstein once said, the clearest form of insanity is "doing the same thing over and over again and expecting different results".I'll show you the tools and habits you need to be more productive. The best thing is: You don't need all of them to start gaining back your time and life. Only doing one or two things consistently every single day will do the job for you. The emphasis is on **consistency**. Don't worry if you miss a day. This is where a lot of people give up.

Look at it like this: If you do it six out of seven days over four to six weeks, that's still better than nothing, and you will see results.

Remember: It's what you do every day that will change your life, not what you do every now and then.

Act on the habits you choose over a period of 30 days and see what happens. I have seen enormous success with my coaching clients, and if you do this, your life will change too!

So how do we improve our productivity? In this book we will look at the usual time management techniques like "setting goals", "getting organized", "prioritize", and "planning and scheduling". You will learn to identify distractions and interruptions and how to deal with them efficiently. We will have a look at what is procrastination and how to overcome it. In the second part I'll tell you about some simple habits to win more time, and in the third part we will look at the most important point: "**The Inner Game of Time Management**" which probably is even more important than the tools and techniques. If your beliefs and attitude are not correct, all of the tools and habits will not be that effective. On the other hand, if your beliefs and attitudes are correct, you will see amazing results.

Sounds good? Then let's get to it!

I

THE BASICS

1

Self-discipline and Commitment

L et's do this! This is the first chapter, because you can only become more productive if you have the necessary discipline and are **committed to find time in your days, no matter what**.

Don't be one of those people who say "I'd like to read more", "I'd like to exercise more", "I'd like to write a book", "I'd like to go out into nature more", and then not do it.

Self-discipline and commitment are character traits that will decide whether you do what you said you would do and go through with it, starting by making a schedule and sticking to it or planning your days ahead. **There's more: It's doing the things you need to do, even if you are not in the mood for it**.

Not very self-disciplined? Don't worry. You can start training your self-discipline from this moment on! It's like a muscle. The more you train it, the better you get.

If your self-discipline is weak right now, start training it by setting yourself small, reachable goals like:

Write a thousand words a day instead of writing a book

Not answering the phone for one hour, one day per week

Not looking at your mobile phone, social networks and emails in the first 90 minutes after waking up… and so on.

It's important that you keep your commitments—with others, but also with yourself.

Not keeping your commitments has a terrible consequence: You lose energy, you lose clarity, and even worse, it affects your self-esteem!

Only make commitments that you really want. That can mean fewer commitments and more "No"s. You're already gaining time… If you commit, keep your commitment— whatever it takes.

Saying "No" is so important, and probably one of the best time management tricks of all; it will get a separate chapter all to itself further ahead.

On to the next chapter!

2

Set Your Productivity Goals

If you are like most people, you overestimate what you can do in a week and underestimate what you can do in month. If you go one step at a time and remain flexible, then over time you can achieve things that you couldn't even imagine before. It's like compound interest. The small steps with time sum up to something really big.

Write down your goals and they will drive you to take the right actions. Having clearly defined goals will be crucial on your way towards more productivity.

Your goals are like a GPS system leading the way. But to be led, first of all you have to know where you want to go!

The first step to achieving your goals is to put them in writing. Until a little more than three years ago I wasn't a big goal setter. I was very skeptical. Then I started writing down my goals and incredible things started to happen. I became a lot more productive and focused and accomplished goals that weren't even imaginable just months before.

There's nothing like committing to your goals, writing them down…and achieving them or even exceeding them. (I wanted to sell 2,500 books in 2015 and sold over 12,000—imagine how I felt…)

Of course, writing your goals down involves a certain risk: suddenly you will be able measure what you achieve and what you don't achieve. Have the courage to do it anyway. It will be worth it!

Why write down your goals?

1) You declare to your mind, that out of the 50,000 to 60,000 thoughts you have a day, THE ONES written down are the most important ones.

2) You start concentrating and focusing on the activities that bring you closer to your goal. While written goals keep you focused on where you want to go, you also start taking better decisions.

3) You can look at your written goals everyday. This forces you to act, and helps you to prioritize your actions for the day by asking yourself questions such as, "In this moment, is doing what I'm doing bringing me closer to

my productivity goals, or should I be doing something else?"

Before starting the goal setting process, you have to be very **clear** about your goals. Be **precise** and formulate each goal as a **positive statement**.

Then break them down into **small, realistic, achievable action steps** and make a list of all the steps that you will take to get there.

Calculate how long it will take you. Set a deadline for each action step and goal. Don't worry if you don't reach the goal by the exact date you set; it's just a way of focusing on the goal and creating a sense of urgency.

Create a clear vision of your goals in your mind. See yourself as already having achieved the goal: How does it feel? How does it look? How does it sound? How does it smell?

Another important point:

When pursuing your goals, reward yourself for the effort put in, and not just for the results. If you won 10 minutes a day, you are improving. 10 minutes a day in four weeks are nearly two and a half hours! That's more than you have now, isn't it?

Some small things that will come in handy:

Put a little card with your time management goals written on it in your wallet and read it four to five times daily. The more the better.

Keep a task list. Put your action steps on it as well as the time it takes to do the task, and put a deadline for each task.

I recommend you to check your goals daily/ weekly and monthly—this will boost your productivity enormously!

3
Plan and Schedule

I'm sure you have heard phrases like "If you spend half of your time planning, you will do everything twice as fast!" or "If you don't know where you are going, you can end up anywhere."

They sound so trivial, but we all know there's some truth to them...and yet...are you planning your days? Or are you just floating, fixing things as they turn up, putting out fires, and doing the same things every day?

The habit of planning alone will probably already completely change your life. It changed mine.

Planning your days, weeks, and even months ahead will help you to put the right priorities in place and plan your important work.

I have become an absolute fan of planning. I plan my coming week regularly on Sunday afternoon and "planning tomorrow today" has gained me a lot of time and peace of mind.

So how do you do this?

Make task lists. Put all of your upcoming tasks on there and assign a time to every single action of that list. Always have the list close by and visible. This will help you stay focused during the day.

Another good idea is to work in blocks of time. I usually work in 90-minute blocks and then take a 30-minute break, or if I'm in flow, three-hour blocks and then a two-hour break.

Ask yourself what are the five things that you want to get done tomorrow?

Choose things and actions that move you closer to the completion of your goals and designate the hours you need to complete each action.

Don't forget to schedule free time, fun time and travel time into your calendar, and always leave a little reserve of time for emergencies that might come up.

Problems that can come up while planning your days and weeks

- You don't have time to plan (half an hour on Sunday afternoon to plan your week can do miracles).

- You are too optimistic with your time and have difficulties in estimating how long your tasks will take. So you always need longer that you scheduled, and this builds up a lot of pressure that you are carrying around with you.
- You don't reserve time for unforeseen emergencies or tasks that come up, and your schedule gets ruined every single day by those events.

Create a daily schedule

Schedule your day: Schedule in buffer time for unexpected things that WILL come up. Reserve blocks of time for your nap, free time and fun time. And remember: Don't be busy—go for results.

Yearly planning

Divide your yearly goals into quarterly goals. What do you have to have accomplished by the end of March in order to be on track to your yearly goals?

Monthly goals

Watch your goals for the week every day. What do you have to accomplish this week to achieve your monthly and quarterly goals?

Book your activities into your calendar

Each evening watch your calendar and see what your goals and actions for the next days are so that the next day you know exactly what to do and get directly to work instead of wasting precious time figuring out what to do.

Keep score

Every now and then check on yourself: What did you get done? Were you doing the things you were supposed to be doing to move closer towards your goals, or were you distracted?

Having a log of what you did will give you an overview of your productivity and also help you to see if the time you give yourself for every task is realistic, or if you are too optimistic in your estimation.

I have a friend who always thinks he can get tasks

done in one hour and then takes two hours to complete them. He not only "loses" one hour for every task—which can easily sum up to three hours a day, but there is also a heavy emotional weight bringing him down; a continuous feeling of not accomplishing stuff which naturally attacks his self-esteem.

One big secret of my productivity success is that I always give myself lots of time for the different tasks. If I think I'll do it in an hour, I'll give myself two hours to finish the task. In comparison to my frustrated friend in the example above, I always have enough time and have experienced the success of finishing tasks earlier, paired with rewards and well-being. You'll hardly ever see me stressed.

You can download my yearly, quarterly, weekly and daily planners from my webpage <u>www.</u>goodhabitsacademy.com along with some other coaching worksheets.

4

Prioritize

Prioritizing actually is quite easy. You just have to separate the important from the unimportant stuff. Or as Victor Küppers, one of the best trainers and speakers in Spain says, "The most important thing is that the most important thing is the most important thing."

Unfortunately, many times emergencies come up that have to be taken care of first.

Asking yourself, "What's my most important task for tomorrow?" will help you get focused and give you a head start getting into action the next morning.

So how can we differentiate between what's urgent, what's important, and what isn't?

There are two helpful approaches when you want to prioritize:

Number one is the "time management matrix" which is usually attributed to Stephen Covey and is also known as Eisenhower's Urgent–Important principle, and number two is "The Pareto principle" which is also known as the 80/20 rule.

The time management matrix

Stephen Covey introduced the idea of determining priorities by using four quadrants. The quadrants allow you to prioritize your tasks in relation to their urgency and importance.

Based on which quadrant you put the task in, you decide if it's something you have to do immediately or if you can postpone it.

	Urgent	**Not Urgent**
Important	**Quadrant I:** Urgent and Important	**Quadrant II:** Not Urgent and Important
Not Important	**Quadrant III:** Urgent and not Important	**Quadrant IV:** Not Urgent and not Important

First of all, we differentiate between important tasks and urgent tasks.

The **important** tasks are those that contribute

directly to the achievement of your goals, while the **urgent** ones are those that require your immediate attention. Not dealing with the urgent issues will cause immediate consequences although or because they are often tied to other people's goals.

Here's a summary of the meaning of each quadrant:

Quadrant 1: Urgent and important

Tasks that could have been foreseen.

It includes only those activities that require your immediate attention like emergencies, extremely important deadlines, pressing problems and last minute preparations. (Could better planning have helped?)

Examples: Crisis, customer service, new business, delayed activities, health problems, paying debts, etc.

Quadrant 2: Not urgent but important

Tasks that don't have a high urgency, but play an important role in the future.

This is where you do your strategic planning, about anything related to education, health, recreation, exercise and career. The tasks here might not be urgent at present, but in the long term this quadrant is where you might want to spend most of your time. **The more time you spend here, the less time you'll have to spend in Quadrant 1 where the stress happens**. The better your planning is in Quadrant 2, the less future tasks will be found in Quadrant 1.

Examples: Preparation, prevention, planning, building relationships, self-development, holidays with the family, important social activities.

Quadrant 3: Urgent but not important

Tasks that are not important, but appear to have high urgency go in this quadrant. Activities in this quadrant are often distractions with high urgency. They don't contribute any value and are rather obstacles than anything else. Minimize, eliminate, delegate or reschedule these tasks.

If caused by another person, decline requests politely if possible. Stress often comes up because we confuse Quadrant 3 tasks with Quadrant 1 tasks. I've had a lot of stressed clients who spent their time in Quadrant 3 thinking they were in Quadrant 1. Once they became aware of the difference between the two, their life improved a lot.

Examples: Interruptions, unproductive meetings,

unnecessary calls, reports, checking mails, redoing work, wasted time with people.

Quadrant 4: Not urgent and not important

If you spend most of your time in this quadrant you either are close to getting fired or very lucky that you aren't. The fourth quadrant contains tasks and activities that are absolute time wasters and do not contribute any value at all. These tasks are plain distractions. Eliminate all tasks from this quadrant or plainly avoid them!

Examples: Surfing the web without any purpose, watching TV or YouTube videos, surfing on Facebook, playing games, chatting and messaging, going shopping etc.

So where can the majority of your tasks and activities, both private and professional, be found? My guess is either Quadrant 1 or 3. Mostly Quadrant 2 is neglected, although for your productivity it is the most important one. You should maximize time spent in Quadrant 2 because the more time you spend in that quadrant, the less you will have to spend in Quadrants 1 and 3—which will boost your productivity enormously. The better you plan your activities and tasks, the less Quadrant 1 activities will there be in the long term.

The time management matrix helps you check whether a certain task or activity brings you closer to your goals. Once that is done, you will know exactly which tasks and activities to prioritize over those that cost you time, but contribute Little, or next to nothing, to your results.

The Pareto principle or the 80/20 rule

The Pareto principle from the beginning of the 20th century was based on the discovery that 20% of the Italian population owned 80% of the land, which seems quite outdated, especially in a world where 1% of the population owns 99% of the wealth, but let's play with it for the heck of it. (Never underestimate the power of a good self-fulfilling prophecy: millions of people believing in the validity of the principle may maintain it is valid even today.)

Pareto researched this ratio and also found it in his garden, where 20% of his tomato plants produced 80% of his tomatoes. I have to admit that I spend 80% of my time in 20% of my house—usually the living and dining room.

Applied to business this would mean (and you can confirm this in your own business and personal life):

80% of your results will come from 20% of your actions

- 80% of your profits come from 20% of your clients
- 80% of your complaints come from 20% of your clients
- 80% of your sales come from 20% of your products

and so on…

So which of your clients bring you 80% of your sales? Wouldn't it be productive to concentrate most of your time on them? What about the 20% of clients that stand for 80% of your complaints? Getting rid of them would surely free up a lot of time that you can save by not having to handle their complaints—as long as they are not the ones who also bring 80% of your benefits, of course!

Same goes for the 20% of your clients that account for 80% of your stress. If they are not bringing in 80% of the money…fire them!

Your business—and your available time—can grow exponentially if you can concentrate on the projects that earn the most money with the least time spent on them.

So sit down and identify—using the Pareto

principle—which projects are holding you back and which ones you should boost. Apply the 80/20 rule to every area of your business and your personal life.

Answer the following questions to yourself:

- Where should you invest more time?
- Where should you invest less time?
- Where are you getting good results investing relatively less time?
- Where are you spending a lot of time and getting few results?

5
Focus

One of the most important habits for improving your productivity is the ability to FOCUS.

When you are focusing, you will get more work done than any other day when you are multitasking.

I don't know who came up with the theory that multitasking is actually good for your productivity, but it's a big lie. Do yourself a favor and stop multitasking right now! You are not gaining time with it; you're actually wasting time shifting from one task to another.

You are much better off doing **one thing at a time!**

The newest studies show that multitasking is actually less productive and that nothing beats doing one thing at a time with a concentrated effort. Some studies even imply that multitasking actually makes you slower and—careful now—dumber!

In any case, even if you think you are multitasking,

you are actually doing one thing at a time, aren't you? You might have five tasks on your hands, but I'm sure you don't do all five things at the same time. You are writing an email. You stop writing it and take a phone call. You hang up and continue writing the email. A colleague comes to you with a question. You stop writing your email and answer the question, and so on. So forget about multitasking. **Focus on doing one thing at a time and do it with concentration!**

Batching

Batching is a great way to increase both your focus and your productivity. It means that you will concentrate only on one task for an hour or two. Do this during the time when you don't allow any interruptions or distractions—no email checking, no notification noises, no surfing the web, etc.

Did you ever notice that you get faster when you do the same thing for an hour? Batching things—like one hour of only writing emails, one hour of only answering calls etc.—is incredibly productive and will help you to do things more quickly because you'll get into the flow of the task and won't lose time in refocusing, like when you are switching between tasks or being interrupted. Analyze your tasks and see which ones you can group together. I usually combine the following tasks: planning, answering emails, reading, writing, phone calls, meetings, housework, shopping, etc.

6

Get Organized

You will earn an hour for every five minutes you spend on organizing. Period.

So you are too busy to get organized, aren't you? You have post-its and mountains of paper all over your table. And if you just had a little bit of time to get organized you would do it, right?

I'm sorry that I have to be the one to tell you, but… it's not that you are too busy to get organized, it's because you are not organized that you are so busy!

Unfortunately, "being busy" doesn't mean that you are getting results! And the one with the messiest table in the office is seldom the one who works hardest.

Studies say that today's executives spend between 30% and 50% of their time pushing around paper in search of the document they need. Scary, isn't it?

So, my overwhelmed worker, go on reading and TRY OUT these little tips, as they can change your life! I have been there and I turned it around using the little tips below:

- Spend the first 15 minutes of your work day prioritizing what to do.
- Spend one hour a week organizing and filing papers. If there is something you can do in less than five minutes, DO IT! If it takes longer, put it onto your to-do or tasks list.
- Spend 15 minutes a day throwing away papers and clearing away your desk. Really throw away everything you don't need.
- Spend the last 15 minutes of your work day to go through your tasks for tomorrow. What's important? What's urgent?
- Bring order into your email inbox and delete old mails that you don't need any more. If you are not sure, print the email out and file it to quiet your conscience.
- As an IT technician once told me, deleting your old emails not only makes you feel lighter, it also saves your company or yourself some money because hundreds or thousands of mails stocked up in you inbox cost a lot more in energy—which translates into higher electricity costs.
- Don't accept any new tasks until you are in control.

- Do the job right the first time, so that it doesn't come back to haunt you and cost you more time later.

Organizing and filing paperwork

Collect all of your paperwork and process it as follows:

- If you need less than five minutes to do it, do it now!
- If you need more time, put it on your task list.
- Once you have completed it, archive it.
- If it's for another person, resend it.
- If it's for later, archive it or throw it away.

(How many files do you have that you saved for later? How many of them do you actually need? None of the above? Throw them away.)

Organizing your email inbox

- If you need less than five minutes to respond, do it now.
- If you can delegate it, delegate it NOW.
- If you need more time to process it, put it on your task list.

- Create folders and move finished tasks into them right away.
- Use your email inbox as a to-do list: Tasks solved get archived and tasks unsolved stay in the inbox.
- If you don't need it for future reference, DELETE it.
- Unsubscribe from every newsletter that you don't need—except from mine. Just kidding. For the sake of your productivity, even unsubscribe from mine, although it would be hard to see you go.

Follow these steps until your email inbox is empty.

If you have a lot of emails, work on the ones from last month and archive the others in a folder named "Old emails".

Your work area

Put everything you need within your reach.

- Keep your folders close by and in order.
- Keep your work surface empty and clean.
- Keep things you need to use close by and in good condition.
- Put things you do not need often in a drawer.

- Keep work trays (Incoming, Outgoing, Pending).
- Put order in your head too. Do this by writing down your thoughts and ideas.
- Take time to organize your workplace every week.

Remember: If you lose five minutes a day looking for stuff, that sums up to 30 hours per year! Having or not having this time makes a lot of difference.

Unclutter. PERIOD.

If you don't use it, it's probably clutter. And clutter needs to go! It's all about energy. What goes for your work goes for your home.

If you have too much stuff that you don't use in your house, it drains your energy! If you have less energy, you become less productive. Start with your cupboard.

Here are some tips:

- If you haven't worn it in a year, you probably won't wear it any more.
- When you think "This will be useful one day" or "This reminds me of good times"—out it goes.
- Marie Kondo, Japanese uncluttering guru, goes

even further: "If it doesn't spark joy, out it goes." I highly recommend her book *The Life-Changing Magic of Tidying Up:The Japanese Art of Decluttering and Organizing*. It changed my life.

When I declutter I usually give stuff away for free. It just makes me feel better, and somehow I think life/God/the universe will reward me for it.

Once you are done with the cupboard, take on the whole bedroom. Later move on to the living room, clean out your garage, and end up cleaning up your entire home and office. Get rid of everything that you don't use any more: clothes, journals, books, CDs, even furniture, and so on. One of my clients decluttered his whole apartment in one weekend. He felt so much better and lighter and got an energy boost that it helped him to reach a whole bunch of his short term goals. He never looked back. When will you start decluttering?

Remember those 30 hours you win if you don't have to search for things? Well, having order at home will save you another 30 hours per year. We already found 60 hours! And counting...

Holy guacamole! It's just the beginning of the book, and we already won around 100 hours a year for you. Please read on anyway. ;-)

Reminder:

Like everything else in this book, saying "That won't work for me" doesn't count as an excuse! Try it for at least two weeks, and if it still doesn't work for you, write me an email and complain to me!

7

Distractions and Interruptions

How focused are you at your work? Or to put it in another way: what's the longest time you have focused on your work without getting distracted or interrupted?

For most people, it's not very long. My guess is that you get distracted every four to five minutes. The tone that notifies you that you just received a new email, the vibrating sound on your mobile that signals to you that somebody just commented on one of your Facebook posts, your mom's calls, WhatsApp or text messages, and so on and on and on.

There are two types of interruptions that knock you off your productivity path day after day: internal and external. It's so important to ban all interruptions and distractions, **because it's not just the interruption or distraction time you lose**, you also lose your focus, and studies show that it takes you 7 to 15 minutes to refocus. Some people even say it takes you 25 minutes to refocus.

How many times do you get distracted or interrupted every day? 10 times?

In the best case scenario, that's 70 minutes you lose, and in the worst case, four hours...

This explains why disciplined and productive people can get done more in a day than other people in a whole week!

If you want to control distractions, you need to develop and build your self-discipline and the ability to let nobody and nothing distract you. But believe me, it's going to be worth it!

Dealing with external interruptions is another ball game and depends, to a large extent, on your ability and willingness to say NO without fear.

A small course in the art of saying "No"

Decide ahead of time how you are going to reject the request for a favor. Practice it! Always be nice and friendly, but firm when telling somebody that you can't help them right away. It's up to you if you want to explain why you are rejecting the person's request for immediate help.

My personal opinion is you don't have to explain anything. Funny enough, I was the guy always giving explanations until one day I didn't feel the need to explain any more. You can always offer other options or alternatives such as, "Sorry I can't help you right now. I could support you for an hour on Friday afternoon." Try to get to an agreement and find acceptable compromises when possible.

If you say "yes" to everything, you will be the busiest person in the office, you will do extra time when your colleagues are going home, and you will get called on Friday nights or on the weekend.

How dare they call you on a Friday night or on weekends! Sorry, it's not *"them"*. It's *you* taking the call and thus indirectly signalling to them, "It's okay to call me whenever you want."

It's you who has to set the limits.

How to deal with external interruptions:

Interruptions by workmates or the boss

Don't consider every petition as urgent. Take your time and think about when it is a good time to act. If it's a valid interruption, schedule it in your task list, but don't let other people's priorities become your priorities. If the petition comes from your boss, tell him or her how making this a priority will affect your other projects and tasks, and renegotiate if necessary.

Keep an "interruptions log" for two weeks and write down who interrupts you.

Interruptions by phone

I know. You have to take every phone call; if not, you will lose the client/sponsor etc. If I got a dollar for every time I've heard this... Yet, after putting a rule into action, I never ever received any complaint about lost clients. In fact, one of my clients even improved his sales and got more clients! You'll read more about him later.

It's okay to not take every call or let calls go to voice mail at least for an hour a day.

They will leave a message or call back and you will win a lot of time, because that hour without interruptions will be your most productive hour every day.

You can also redirect it to a colleague who'll nicely tell the caller that you are in a meeting, and take a message. Schedule a specific time for your outgoing calls and batch them to gain additional time.

Avoid distractions

"The major difference between successful people and the unsuccessful is their ability to not get distracted."

I know a lot of people who think and tell me that they are sooooo busy, work lots of overtime, and don't have any idea how and where to win time.

Once we look a little bit closer at their routine, we notice that they are checking their email every 20 minutes, getting notifications from people who saw their stuff on Facebook or Twitter, and are checking every new email that comes in every 5 minutes. Apart from this they are surfing on the internet and watching YouTube videos and cat photos on Facebook.

The solution

Close your internet browser.

- Redirect your phone or take it off the hook.
- Turn off your mobile phone or at least turn the sound and notification sounds off. (I usually put my phone on airplane mode in order to

work productively and without interruptions or distractions.)

- Close your email and don't check your emails regularly. (Three times a day for half an hour should be enough.)
- Log out of your social media networks.
- Set fixed times to be on Facebook, Twitter etc. and stick to them.
- Close your office door.

Doing some of these things means an hour or two of time without being distracted by text messages or phone calls. Try it!

Once you start it, you'll love it. You'll notice that you'll get more things done than ever before.

Just one or two hours a day can do miracles for your productivity.

If you are working from home, think very well who you let distract you. The person who wants to have coffee with you or take you to the mall will probably not be paying your bills at the end of the month when you wish back those hours that you lost being distracted and not doing what had to be done.

Another advice…don't turn on the TV. You know it. Once it's on—gone is your productivity.

You can use the TV as a motivation, though: "If I get done what I planned for today I'm going to reward myself with my favorite series."

Reward yourself

Reward yourself when you get things done!

This can actually increase your focus and productivity. Setting up a reward can get you motivated to get things done fast.

For example: If I work on my book from 7 to 10 AM, I usually give myself a two-hour break to check my private Facebook account and watch one episode of my favorite series.

But I can only get this reward if I write and produce until 10 AM sharp.

I usually reward myself in the following way: Meeting friends, taking a power nap, watching a movie or TV series, enjoying a nice bubble bath, walking on the beach, going to the beach bar and having a coffee, reading a good book, playing an hour on my Xbox (needs a lot of discipline...ONE hour—not more...), a guided meditation.

Distractions are everywhere. You just can't get rid of them. What you can do is get really good at recognizing them. Once you are aware of them, you can take action to refocus.

Here's a list of the typical distractions that will keep you from being productive. Which ones are you guilty of?

- Watching TV
- Playing video games (or mobile games)
- Letting people interrupt you
- Checking emails every time you get one
- Watching your phone all the time (calls, texts, apps)
- Looking out the window
- Social networking
- Surfing on websites
- Looking at photos
- "Researching"
- Eating and drinking
- Worrying
- Thinking of the past or daydreaming

8

Procrastination

If you are working the whole day, but at the end of the day are not getting things done, or seeing any results of your work, there is a high chance that you are procrastinating the important stuff.

No worries. Everybody is procrastinating every now and then. It happens to the best of us.

Procrastination is a major thief of time and the goal is to minimize procrastination so that we can get more things done.

Read closely now—you might be procrastinating without even knowing it. Once you become aware that you are procrastinating and know the methods that you are using to do it, you can catch yourself and take countermeasures like outsourcing tasks you don't like to do at all or not giving in to cheap excuses of your "inner saboteur".

So how do you notice that you are procrastinating?

- You are avoiding something that should be done.
- You are putting off tasks, hoping that they magically get better without us actually doing anything about them. (Usually things don't get better on their own…and a lot of times they will get worse.)
- You are doing things that don't need to be done right now instead of doing what you are supposed to be doing—and it doesn't matter if those things you are doing are more or less important!

Yes. You read right. Even doing something that is more important than what we are supposed to be doing is procrastination.

Procrastination comes in a wide variety of forms:

- Getting distracted
- Putting off tasks
- Waiting until a task is perfect in order to complete it
- Leaving everything till the very last minute

Are you a delayer, a perfectionist or easily distractible? The most common reason for procrastination is some kind of fear: fear of failure, fear of being judged, even fear of success, to name a few.

Even if we procrastinate because we are lazy or because we lack motivation, there might be an underlying fear responsible for it.

Sometimes feeling overwhelmed is the reason we procrastinate.

Excuses can be a form of procrastination

Whenever you use the following excuses, watch yourself very closely! You might be procrastinating, saying:

- "I'm too tired."
- "I don't have time for it right now."
- "I need a break."
- "I don't feel like doing that now, I'll feel more like it later."
- "It's too late to start this today, I'll do it tomorrow first thing."

Whenever I catch myself talking like this, I watch very closely what am I doing at that exact moment. What task am I doing, and why does my mind want to distract me from it?

I use the trigger as fuel to do the task anyway, telling myself, **"If my mind wants to trick me into** procrastinating this task, it must be really important, so I will stay here and finish it now**," instead of giving in to the temptation of watching senseless videos on YouTube, cat photos on Facebook, or cleaning up my room (not so senseless, but a great way to procrastinate).

So when I'm on a task and suddenly feel the urge to do dishes and clean up the house, I clearly identify that as an intent to procrastinate and finish the task at hand.

Unfortunately I wasn't that smart 20 years ago when I had this intense urge to clean up my apartment every time I was studying for an exam. Funnily, this urge always showed up during exam time—never during the rest of the year. So twice a year my apartment was super-tidy while I failed exams…

The easily distractible lose themselves in games, TV, on the internet, or going to the mall.

If you catch yourself playing Candy Crush, you might just want to have a look at the task that you should be doing instead, and analyze why you are not doing it.

Here are some more procrastination excuses, and how to deal with them:

1) **"I don't have enough time."**
That's why you bought this book in the first place,

isn't it? I hope you already found more time. Did you start making lists? When you have your task list, start working. Action is always and by far the best antidote to procrastination.

2) **"I have too many things on my plate."**

Who doesn't? There are always a lot of things to do, and it probably will never stop, but which are your priorities? Which tasks will give you the best results?

3) **"I can't decide what to start with."**

Indecision arises when you are overwhelmed by too many options, and don't know what to start with. The best is to start with the biggest, most overwhelming decision to take.

4) **"It's not perfect yet."**

This is one of the most dangerous excuses! It can be used to procrastinate forever!

We don't see perfectionists as procrastinators, because they seem to be proactive and efficient. But are they really? If you are not finishing your book, your webpage, or your project because it's not "perfect" yet, then you, my dear, might suffer from "paralysis by analysis" and are a procrastinator. For me, the best tip I ever got was **"Done is better than perfect."**

Watch very closely how much of a difference putting in more effort really makes. Will your search for perfectionism steal away time that you need for other tasks?

A good trick for the perfectionists among us is to calculate how much your time is worth in money and then decide if what you are doing is beneficial. If you work 10 hours instead of 2 to finish a task, you are losing money. Especially when the additional 8 hours only add little to the result.

Choose to finish the project NOW, and then improve it along the way. Like, for example, software companies do, right?

5) **"It's not the right time, I'm waiting for the right moment."**
Oh dear, oh dear. If I had a dollar for every time I heard this one…
If you are waiting for the right moment to start your new business, launch your new product or do your live event, **you might as well wait forever**, **because the right moment never comes.**

And neither does the sign from the universe you are waiting for. Maybe the universe is sending you signs all the time, and you just can't see them. There is no "right time" to do something, or better said, **the right time to do something is always NOW.**

I don't know who said it first, but the term "waiting for the right time to start something is like waiting in your driveway for all the traffic lights to turn green before going for a drive" has it about right. Usually procrastination ends in guilt, anxiety, self-loathing, or even depression, and it's damaging to the procrastinator's self-esteem and inner peace. This is a price far too high to pay.

The worst thing is, you lose twice. You don't do what needs to be done, but you also can't enjoy the activity you're doing instead of what needs to be done because of a bad conscience or because you are feeling guilty.

Become a doer! Do what needs to be done and afterwards enjoy the rewards without having a black cloud hanging over your head.

Solutions

- Be absolutely honest with yourself. If tempted to procrastinate, ask yourself, "What price am I paying for procrastinating this task?"
- Dive straight in. (Action is the best antidote to procrastination.)Focus on the results you'll get by

doing the task you are tempted to leave for later.

- Focus on the rewards.
- Work with others (coach, accountability partner).
- Set yourself deadlines.
- Analyze, divide and conquer tasks.
- Do the most uncomfortable task first thing in the morning.
- Focus on the task that brings in money.

II

PRODUCTIVITY HABITS

1

Do It NOW!

That unwritten email, the conversation with that annoying colleague or customer, the talk with your boss about that raise. Do it NOW. This habit will help you to really get stuff done. I'm sure you know the best time to finish a task is always NOW.

Do yourself a favor and stop the procrastination. It only causes anxiety! And most of the time you will find that things that you procrastinated for days causing you anxiety and a bad conscience are actually done in an hour or so and afterwards you feel so much lighter because you can forget about it.

Whatever it is that you have on your mind right now, don't start tomorrow or next week! Start NOW! I promise you—in a year you will be happy that you started today!

Same goes for every task that takes you less then five minutes to finish, like answering short emails (batch it if you can), calling your mother back, calling your phone company, booking that dentist appointment, etc.

Do it now!

Do the uncomfortable tasks first thing in the morning. I know it's tough, but it will improve the quality of the rest of your day. Because—as I mentioned before—if you postpone it, you will carry it around with you all day anyway, and your conscience will weigh you down. Do it now and forget about it.

The afternoon or other low-energy phases are good for doing simple stuff like organizing daily mail, cleaning your desk, easy reading, filling in excel sheets, following up, filing, etc.

2
Work against Time

A great productivity habit is to develop a sense of urgency and to work against time. Set yourself deadlines. If you have enough self-discipline to take your own deadlines seriously, fantastic! If not, include other people that you don't want to let down.

Coaching, for example, is so effective and successful because the majority of clients don't want to let their coaches down. They do their stuff, and thus make progress from week to week towards their goals.

Back to time management...

Some people say you should punish yourself for not meeting your deadlines: like not watching your favorite series on TV or not going out. If you have read my other books you know I'm not a big fan of any kind of self-punishment.

Why not reward yourself for making the deadline with watching your favorite TV series or going to the movies? A little change in perspective, but a whole new outlook.

Two completely different approaches to the same result…The choice is yours!

The last day before vacation

Remember the last day before vacation when you suddenly get everything done? Why? Because it has to be done. Suddenly tasks get finished that haven't been finished for weeks. You have to take tough decisions then and there, and can't afford the luxury of procrastinating.

So why not pretend every day to be the last day before your vacation?

Parkinson's law

Parkinson's law states that "Work expands so as to fill the time available for its completion" which means whatever time you have to complete a project, you will need that time to complete it.

That's why you usually finish a two-week project on the evening of Day 13, and if you had three weeks for the same project, you'd finish it on the evening of Day 20.

Another reason is that deadlines force you to focus more on the task at hand. You concentrate on the essential, start cutting out any other superfluous activities, and get things done.

It's when you have a deadline that you start keeping your emails and phone calls short, and suddenly win a lot of time. I see it over and over again: people tell me they don't have time, but then they spend hours on the phone.

I once worked with a colleague who worked a lot of overtime and never got her work done on time. Looking closer at her work process—she was a logistics manager—I noticed that when she booked a transport she called and stayed on the phone for 20 minutes with every freight forwarder to talk about her life when an email would have done the job. She talked to about five freight forwarders a day… You do the math.

Now don't misunderstand me; it's great and necessary to build great relationships with your suppliers, but if you are complaining about not having time…don't stay on the phone for 20 minutes. Make it 10 or even better—5 minutes!

Phone calls

When you get called, get to the point quickly—it's best to already have an exit strategy when you pick up the phone…be polite but show that you don't have time to waste.

For example, tell your counterpart right at the beginning, "Hi! Nice to hear from you. I'm just preparing for an important reunion. I have five minutes. What can I do for you?" Or something like that. It works. People get to the point much quicker when you start like this.

Email templates might be another possibility to win some minutes here and there. These minutes will add up.

Challenges

Set yourself little challenges such as "I'll get this done in one hour" and see how you are doing.

The curse of "being busy"

Many people are using the "I'm busy" excuse for never finishing things:

"I have to finish my webpage. It will be great, but I'm so busy and don't have time to do it."

"I have this great book inside me, but I'm busy and don't have time to write…"

"I have this great business idea, but I'm so busy I don't have time to look for alternatives and will stay in my dead-end job a little longer until I have time to send some CVs."

Stop using time as an excuse and start using your time better! Learn to get the important things done and stop wasting time doing useless stuff (a.k.a being busy) until you have built up some time reserves.

As I said before, being busy doesn't mean that you are being productive and getting results.

Pomodoro technique

I don't know what impresses me more: the simplicity and efficiency of this technique or the fact that entire books have been written on how to set a timer to 25 minutes, work 25 minutes, and then take a 5-minute break.

Basically it's another approach to the things mentioned earlier. Work 25 minutes **without interruptions**, then take a 5-minute break. After four pomodoros (2 hours), take a longer break of 15 to 30 minutes.

The Pomodoro technique should help you to focus and reduce the impact of external and internal distractions.

The fun starts when a whole department starts applying this technique. I've heard that productivity in such a department literally explodes. If you have experience with the Pomodoro technique, please let me know. I'm always interested in real-life examples.

3

Develop a Morning Ritual

This is my favourite moment of each day and my morning ritual contributed a lot, if not everything, to my well-being, wealth and productivity. This ritual alone might solve all of your time management problems.

One of the most important moments of your day is the 30 minutes after you wake up. This is when your subconscious is very receptive, so it's of big importance what you do in this time.

The way you start your day will have a huge impact on how the rest of your day develops. I'm sure you have had days which have started off on the wrong foot and from then on it got worse and worse—or the opposite when you woke up with that feeling that everything would go your way and then it did.

That's why it's very important to begin your day well. Most of us just get into a rush from the minute after waking up and that's how our days unfold. No wonder most people run around stressed nowadays. What would getting up half an hour or an hour earlier every morning do for you?

What if instead of hurrying and swallowing down your breakfast or even having it on the way to work, you get up and take half an hour for yourself? Maybe you even create a little morning ritual with a 10- or 15-minute meditation? Do you see what this could do for your life if you made it a habit? Here are some activities for the morning ritual. Give it a shot!

- Think positive: Today is going to be a great day!
- Remember for 5 minutes what you are grateful for.
- 15 minutes of quiet time.
- Imagine the day is about to start going very well.
- Go over your schedule for today. What's important? What has to get done?
- Watch a sunrise.
- Go running or take a walk.
- Write in your journal.

The last half an hour of your day has the same importance! The things you do in the last half an hour before sleeping will remain in your subconscious during your sleep. So then it's time to do the following:

- Write in your journal again.
- Now is the time for reflecting on your day. What did you do great? What could you have done even better?
- Plan tomorrow today. What are the most important things you want to get done tomorrow?
- Make a to-do list for the next day.
- Visualize your ideal day.
- Read some inspirational blogs, articles or chapters of a book.
- Listen to music that inspires you.

I highly recommend that you DO NOT WATCH NEWS or MOVIES that agitate you before you go to sleep. This is because when you are falling asleep you are highly receptive to suggestions. That's why it's a lot more beneficial to listen to or watch positive material. The planning ahead of your day and the list of things to do can bring you immense advantages and time saving. The things you have to do will already be in your subconscious plus you will get to work very focused the next day if you already know what your priorities are.

4
Say No

This is one of those habits that will improve your productivity (and your life) a lot.

Did you know that the most successful people say no to nearly everything?

Here's what happened to me:

When I stopped wanting to please others and started being myself, a lot of it came with the word "No". Every time you say "No" when you mean "No", you are actually saying "Yes" to yourself!

Before learning to say "No", I often accepted invitations I didn't want to or went to events I didn't enjoy. The result was I was there physically but mentally I was in another place, and honestly, I was not the best company. Not to mention that I could have used the time for more important stuff.

If you say yes to everything, you will never have enough time, because other people will decide your schedule, and not you.

When I decided that a "Yes" is a "Yes" and a "No" is a "No", I felt much better. I accepted a lot less invitations (this already makes up for a lot of time) and although telling "NO" was hard at the beginning, the result was that when I accepted invitations to events or going out, I was fully there.

In my work life, the impact was even greater. Guess what happened when I said yes to every favor I was asked for…? I ended up being totally overwhelmed at work, because I was asked for a lot of favors and took on a lot of extra tasks—usually work nobody else wanted to do.

It took me a while to put my foot down, but finally I said "Enough". From then on, my first answer to all requests for favors was "NO! Sorry. Can't do it. Very busy at the moment!"

By starting to say "No" often, you will improve your work and personal life a lot and actually free up a lot of time.

But make sure you say "NO" without feeling guilty! You can explain to the person in question that it's not anything personal against them, but for your own well-being. You can still do your colleagues a favor, but only if you have enough time, and decide to. If you do this, you will find that suddenly you are in the driver's seat.

Now you might say: "But Marc, what you are suggesting here is not what teamwork looks like." And you are right. But neither is going at half power knowing your coworker will save the day for you...I know you know that guy...he or she is in every office.

In one phrase:

Of course you can still do favors for your colleagues—and you should but under your conditions!

If I was up for it I would mention to the colleague in question that I'm only doing a favor, and in no case do I want to end up doing the job.

Selfish? Yes! But keep in mind who the most important person in your life is. That's right! YOU are the most important person in your life! You have to be well! Only if you are well yourself can you be good to others, and from this level on you can contribute to others, but first be well yourself. You can always buy some time and say "maybe" at first, until you come to a definite decision. Life gets a lot easier if you start saying "No"!

5

Arrive 10 Minutes Early

Yes. This is a time management and productivity trick. Well, kind of a mix. It might be more of a stress relief technique. Anyway, it has done me so much good that I want to share it with you.

Being early for your appointments will take a lot of stress off your shoulders because you won't feel a rush all the time. It might also give you some time to answer a quick email or a phone call.

I noticed it especially when coming in to work 10 minutes earlier. I had time to sit down, relax, look at my task list and then go full speed ahead into my work day, when before I used to arrive just in time or maybe even late and was then stressed out all the time from the first minute at work. If you're not doing it already, try it out and let me know how it works for you.

Being 10 minutes early is also a good habit for business meetings, lunches or dinners.

There's a French proverb that is always on my mind that says, "While we keep a man waiting, he reflects on our shortcomings."

Punctuality is a sign of discipline and respect for others. Without it, you might come across as slightly offensive, even if you are the nicest person in the world. Of course there are cultural differences. For example, while in Mexico and Spain people are very relaxed about punctuality, in Germany not being punctual is seen as highly unprofessional and might ruin your chances in any endeavor.

I have made being 10 minutes early to every appointment a habit—not to be especially polite, but instead, I do it for myself.

Those 10 minutes will make you feel a lot better and will give you a lot of peace of mind. When you arrive at a place, you aren't in a rush, and you actually have 10 minutes to compose your thoughts and prepare for the interview or meeting. Instead of feeling rushed arriving at the last minute, you'll feel very relaxed.

Being 10 minutes early shows professionalism and politeness. Try it and see for yourself if it adds to your life or not!

6

Underpromise, Overdeliver

This is another biggie. A great time management technique that changed my professional life in an extraordinary manner and reduced stress at work to virtually zero!

Most of my stress at work came from deadlines, and I, or we as an enterprise, were always struggling, which made those days when our products were shipped to the clients—which was every day during high season— horrible and very stressful.

We were always just in time or sometimes maybe a couple of hours late and I had to calm down angry and sometimes hysterical clients...until I started to underpromise:

I figured out that over 90% of our late deliveries were just a question of a couple of hours, so I got permission from my boss and started my own delivery schedule that only I had access to.

If production gave me a delivery date of April 5th, I told the client April 10th. So if we delivered on April 7th, instead of an angry client threatening to fine or sue us for being two days late, I suddenly had extremely grateful clients who thanked me for delivering three days early. Within a short time we reduced late deliveries from nearly 50% to virtually 0% over the next three years.

I found out later that a great side effect of controlling our own deadlines was a diminished risk of coronary heart disease by a whopping 50%—at least. (A study found that people who have little control over deadlines imposed by other people have a 50% higher risk of coronary heart desease.)

You can apply this to your entire life. When your boss gives you a project that takes you three days, you could tell him or her that you are going to need five days. If you have completed it after four days you'll come off as a great worker, and if you take a little longer, you are still on time. For me this worked out great. In my whole life as an employee I never had to stay a weekend at the office.

Of course, you have to customize this technique and adapt it to your workplace and environment. I don't want you to get fired for lying to your boss...

If you are struggling with deadlines at work, trying

this and making it a habit is definitely worth a shot.

I also apply it to my private life: If I know that it takes me half an hour to get to a meeting place, I tell my friends I'll be there in an hour, and by showing up half an hour early I see happy faces and convey to the people I meet, "You are important to me, I rushed to see you."

I don't know about your friends and family, but mine prefer this a thousand times over telling somebody, "I'll be there in half an hour" and then showing up after an hour.

7

Turn Off Your Phone

Do you think you have to pick up your phone each time it rings? Well...don't!

Your phone is supposed to be for YOUR convenience, not for those who call you. Give yourself the freedom to continue doing whatever you are doing and let calls go to voice mail every now and then.

I know. I know... You might lose a client. Every single one of my clients thought that.

Guess what: You probably won't lose the client.

Leave a nice message on your voice mail on the lines of the good old "Sorry I'm busy and can't take your call right now. I'll call you back as soon as possible."

If it's important, they will call again. Or they will leave a message. Or you'll see their number on your display and call them. The only thing that's really bad is not calling them back right after you have finished what you are doing, or even forgetting them.

One of my clients, a very stressed sales manager, let's call him Steve, came to me at the edge of being seriously burnt out. He received 60 to 80 calls a day and didn't have time to do his real job, which was selling his product and visiting customers, because he was on the phone all the time fixing everyone's problems and continuously putting out fires.

I laid out all of the different time management tools for him that you find in this book. He had to choose the one that fit best for him.

He decided to let calls go to voice mail for at least an hour every day and changed the message of his voice mail. "Hi. I can't get to the phone right now. I'll call you back as soon as I can. If it's urgent, send me a Whatsapp message." That's it.

The first two weeks there were no big changes. In the third week he suddenly received only half the calls, and by the time he called back, 80% of the problems people had called for in the first place were fixed.

After a month he was relaxed. He thought he might have received fewer calls because vacation time was close by or work was slow.

Three months later he had to admit to himself that he had done it! He was in control of his time. He also improved his free time with his family on the weekends because he wasn't thinking about work all the time and had time to think about fun stuff to do with his family.

Further, he went on to break his sales record for that year (2015) and the next (2016). He expects to increase his sales by another 20%…if he decides to stay in his job, that is, because Steve got a very good offer from a big competitor to join their sales team! **All this nine months after his first step: changing the message of his voice mail. Mind-boggling!**

Not picking up the phone every time it rings and telling myself "They will call again" has worked for me for years, and I think I didn't lose a lot of clients by it. I WON a lot of time, though. I also learnt that if it's a really important call, the caller will not give up and probably call like eight times within three minutes…

8

Spend Time with Your Family

"Family is not an important thing, it's everything," says Michael J. Fox. Be smart and listen to the man who went to the future and back three times.

This is a very important habit. **There are various studies that prove that the biggest and most powerful predictors of success and happiness in our life are our relationships**!

Nevertheless, when I interview leaders and executives, most of the time what comes up is that they just cannot (?) spend a lot of time with their families or that when they are stressed, the first hours to cut are the ones they spend with their family and friends—when they should be doing exactly the opposite.

Value your family and friends. They are your constant source of love and mutual support, which increases your self-esteem, boosts your self-confidence and—as I just said—even makes you happier and more successful.

In Bronnie Ware's book *The Top Five Regrets of the Dying: A Life Transformed by the Dearly Departed*, one of the top regrets of the dying is to **not have spent more time with their families and to have spent too much time at the office**!

Don't become one of them, and start making time for your family NOW! And if you are with the family… do everybody a favor and BE FULLY PRESENT.

Believe it or not, this habit will also make you more productive. It's not only about the work—it's also about how you spend your free time. But as with everything in this book, you can only find out if you put it into practice.

9
Take Time Off

You didn't expect that here, did you? Same as taking a power nap, taking time off actually boosts your productivity instead of damaging it!

With the stressful, fast-paced life that we are living, it's more important than ever to slow down your pace of life and take a break!

Take some time off. Recharge your batteries by being around nature.

Start by scheduling some relaxation time into your weekly schedule which, by now, you are hopefully making time for.

If you dare, completely disconnect from the Internet, TV, and your electronic games for a whole weekend. If that "scares" you, start with a Saturday morning, then a whole Saturday, and then the whole weekend.

One of my best vacations ever was being on a houseboat in the Midi Channel in the south of France.

No mobile phone, no Internet, no TV. Only ducks. The boat's top speed was 8 km/hr 5 miles/hr) so we were literally "forced" to slow down.

There's few things more relaxing than a couple of six-year-olds riding their bikes overtaking you on the bike paths on the side of the channel while you are floating.

The villages you pass by are sometimes so small, that they don't even have a supermarket. So the whole trip comes down to the one and only simple question: "Where will we get food?"

No worries! There is always a restaurant close by, but the charming thing is to cook your own meals on the boat and have dinner at the harbour watching the sunset or just being around nature. Once we even had dinner in the middle of a vineyard! Priceless!

So is it to walk into a tiny French village in the morning and get your baguette for breakfast from the only bakery in town. We got up at sunrise and went to bed two chess matches after sunset. Or you might say "We got up with the ducks and went to sleep with the ducks."

Take time off and connect with nature! It doesn't have to be a long trip. Walk in the woods, on the beach, or in a park whenever you get the chance, and observe how you feel afterwards. Or just lie down on a bench or on the grass and contemplate the blue sky. When was the last time you walked barefoot on grass or on a beach? Did you get an idea of how important, relaxing and reenergizing taking some time off is for you? I hope so! Go put it into practice. You will double your productivity with this habit!

10
Take a Power Nap

There's nothing like a power nap! It's scientifically proven that a power nap at midday reenergizes, refreshes and increases your productivity.

I made my nap a daily habit. That allows me to sleep around six hours a night without worrying about my sleep. I know that come afternoon I will get my 45–90 minute nap.

Since I changed my sleep rhythm I'm much clearer, more focused, and yes…more awake.

During my most stressful period at my old job I started taking a power nap, and the change was extraordinary. I was far less stressed and a lot calmer while being yelled at by angry clients and much more concentrated and efficient in finding solutions.

For a while, I slept for 25–30 minutes on a bench in a park close by, and later I just put two chairs together in the office and slept there.

It felt as if my work day suddenly had two halves, and midday was halftime. I started the "second half" always fresh and I also performed a lot more productively because the typical tiredness after lunch between 2 and 5 P.M. was gone.

As absurd as it sounds, you will find more time if you nap 30–40 minutes every day. You will be better rested and thus much more productive.

11

Maximize Lost Time

If time is what we most want, why are we using it so badly?

How much time are you spending in the car or public transport on your way to work every day? Statistics say it's between 60 and 90 minutes per work day! That means in a month we are talking between 20–30 hours.

Who said, "I don't have enough time"? We just found you another 20–30 hours to read (when on a bus or train), or listen to audio books in your car.

What if you really spent that time listening to empowering CDs, MP3s, or reading inspirational books instead of listening to the negative news from the radio or reading about it in the newspaper?

How much you could learn in one year! It would be like going to university again!

Do you maximize your "lost time"?

I work a lot on the train, and wrote half of my last book *From Jobless to Amazon Bestseller* on the train, and while writing this chapter I'm actually on the train between Barcelona and Premia de Mar where I live!

Another thing I do on public transport is listening to motivational speeches, or guided meditations, and connecting on social media.

The supermarket queue is also a great time to go through your social media or answer some quick emails—all the stuff I don't do when I'm productive.

When I'm on the train surfing on Facebook or the web, depending on what I'm doing, I often even credit it to myself as work time.

Other possibilities are: listening to a webinar while doing the dishes, watching TV while folding your clothes, and many more.

So now the question is: How will you maximize your lost time?

12
Keep a Journal

This is another one of these habits that will have a crucial impact on your productivity. Write in your journal and reflect on your days.

It's about taking a couple of minutes at the end of your day to get some perspective, relive the happy moments, reflect on the work done, and write everything down in your journal.

By doing this, you will receive an extra boost of happiness, motivation and self-esteem every morning and evening. Writing in your journal has the positive side effect that just before sleeping, you will be concentrating on positive things, which has a beneficial effect on your sleep and your subconscious mind.

Journaling will shift your focus to the positive things of the day, and gratitude. It will make your brain scan the last 24 hours for positive things, the result of which will be a higher level of happiness and optimism for you which…surprise, surprise…as countless studies from the field of positive psychology prove, will make you more productive! Those studies show that happy people are around 20% more productive than their neutral or unhappy coworkers.

For my clients and also for myself, this little exercise has led to enormous changes in my well-being.

Make an effort to answer the following questions each night before sleeping, and write them in your journal:

- What am I grateful for? (Write 3–5 points.)
- What 3 things have made me happy today?
- What 3 things did I do particularly well today?
- How could I have made today even better
- What is my most important goal for tomorrow?

Don't worry if the words don't flow right away when you start this exercise. Like all other things, you will get better with practice. If you face a block and can't think of anything, just hold on for five minutes longer. Write what comes to mind without thinking, and don't judge it. Don't worry about your style or mistakes. Just write! Do this every day for a month and observe the changes that take place!

By the way, these five questions also make for a great conversation with your spouse and kids over dinner!

13

Stop Watching TV

Y ou want to gain time fast, don't you? Here is the tip that will let you gain a lot of time!

How many hours a week do you sit in front of the "box"? The average American or European spends 4–5 hours a day in front of the TV!

That's between 28 and 35 hours a week! Here, you have it. You just won 20 hours, supposing you cut down you daily TV time to an hour. Yes, and count in YouTube also.

Apart from gaining time, there is another beneficial side effect! TV is one of the biggest energy robbers, if not the no. 1!

Do you ever feel renewed or reenergized after watching TV? Turn off your television!

Why would you expose yourself to so much negativity? Don't expose yourself too much to the garbage that is out there on TV. Substitute your habit of watching TV for a healthier habit like taking a walk, spending more time with your family, or reading a good book.

I stopped watching the news many years ago when I became aware that while on the train to work I got upset over things heard and seen on the morning news, and I thought to myself, "I can't go to my stressful workplace being already stressed, simply because of what politician A said or banker B did or because there is a war in C." Just one week after I stopped watching the news I felt a lot better! Don't believe me? Just try it for yourself! Don't watch the news for a week and see how you feel.

You will still be up to date with the "important stuff", because your family, friends and colleagues will keep you updated. Just choose and be selective about how much garbage you expose your mind to.

And nope—you won't become ignorant because you stop watching TV. **A recent study even shows the opposite! People who don't watch TV are actually better judges of reality than people who are influenced by the daily news programs. Now that is NEWS, isn't it?**

If you need more reasons to stop watching television, read one of the great books that are out there about how the media manipulates us and how nearly everything is fake! Control the information that you are exposed to.

Make sure it adds to your life. Instead of watching trash TV, watch a documentary or a comedy. Instead of listening to the news in your car, listen to an audio book or motivational speeches.

III

THE INNER GAME OF PRODUCTIVITY

1

Know Yourself

The first step before changing your life is becoming aware of where you are and what's missing. You might remember this questionnaire from my book *30 Days— Change Your Habits, Change Your Life*. The reason is simple. Every process of self-improvement—**including your productivity**—starts with getting to know yourself better. Whatever your goals and dreams are, you won't get around answering these questions to yourself honestly. So, the earlier you start—like NOW—the better.

This questionnaire is also the starting point of all my coaching processes. So even if you did it before, please take some time to answer the following questions.

What are your dreams in life?

_____

_____

At the end of your life, what do you think you would most regret not having done for yourself?

If time and money were not factors, what would you like to do, be, or have?

What motivates you in life?

What limits you in life?

What have been your biggest wins in the last 12 months?

What have been your biggest frustrations in the last 12 months?

What do you do to please others?

What do you do to please yourself?

What do you pretend not to know?

What has been the best work that you have done in your life until today?

How exactly do you know that this was your best work

How do you see the work you do today in comparison to what you did five years ago? What's the relationship between the work you do now and the work you did then?

What part of your work do you enjoy the most?

What part of your work do you enjoy the least

What activity or thing do you usually postpone?

What are you really proud of?

How would you describe yourself?

_____

_____

What aspects of your behavior do you think you should improve?

_____

_____

At this moment in time, how would you describe your commitment level to making your life a success?

_____

_____

At this moment in time, how would you describe your general state of well-being, energy and self-care?

_____

_____

At this moment in time, how would you describe how much fun or pleasure you are experiencing in your life?

_____

_____

If you could put one fear behind you once and for all, what would it be?

_____

_____

In what area of your life do you most want to have a true breakthrough?

_____

_____

2
Believe

"Be not afraid of life. Believe that life is worth living, and your belief will help create the fact."

Science is now catching up with what William James knew a long time ago: Your beliefs create your reality. Period. You create what you believe, and your world is only your interpretation of the reality.

In other words, you don't see the world how it is, but how you were conditioned to see it, and your perception is only an approximation of reality.

Your maps of reality determine the way you act more than reality itself, and each one of us sees the world through the lenses of their own beliefs. If you believe you don't have enough time, imagine what will happen…

This is not just hocus-pocus. There are countless studies in the field of Positive Psychology and Medicine that prove the power of your beliefs such as the

Placebo Effect, the Pygmalion Effect and Self-fulfilling prophecies.

These studies show that the Placebo Effect is 55–60% as effective as medicine. For example, in an experiment with poison ivy mentioned by *The New York Times* in 1998, researchers rubbed the arms of their subjects with a harmless plant and told them it was poison ivy. Following that, all of the 13 subjects showed the typical symptoms of poison ivy rash! When they rubbed their arms with REAL poison ivy and told the subjects that it was just a harmless plant, only two of the participants showed symptoms!

They drew the following conclusions:

1. Your belief becomes a self-fulfilling prophecy.
2. Our brains are organized to act on what we **expect** will happen next.

But it gets even better! In the late 1960s, Robert Rosenthal and Leonore Jacobson did the following experiment in an elementary school. They gave intelligence tests to the students to research their academic potential.

Then they told the teachers that the data had identified some students as academicsuperstars. Further they told the teachers that they should not disclose the results, or treat these students differently, and to drive their point home, they added that the teachers would be observed!

At the end of the year, they repeated the test and the identified students had extraordinary results. Not a surprise, you might think. The fun thing is that the students were absolutely average and ordinary and randomly picked by the researchers for the first test!

This is proof of the Pygmalion Effect which states that **our belief in a person's potential brings that potential to life!** This goes for other areas of your life too. Your expectations about your colleagues, spouses or children can make these expectations a reality…so you better always expect the best from others!

Robert Dilts defines beliefs as judgments and assessments about ourselves, others and the world around us. A belief is a habitual thought pattern. Once a person believes something is true (whether it's true or not), he or she acts as if it were—collecting facts to prove the belief even if it's false.

Depending on your belief system, you live your life one way or another.

So, to finally find time you also have to change your belief that you don't have time! Once you start believing that you have time, you'll start finding it everywhere.

As I mentioned before, your beliefs are like a self-fulfilling prophecy. They work like this:

Your beliefs influence your emotions, your emotions influence your actions, and your actions influence your RESULTS!

I've worked with people who had all the time in the world and still couldn't see it. They were convinced that they had no time at all while they spent hours browsing the internet, watching videos on YouTube, or playing games.

You not having time is a reflection of your beliefs, thoughts and expectations of you not having time. So if you want to change that, you first have to change your patterns of thinking.

Remember that for many decades it was thought impossible that a man could run a mile under four minutes. There were even scientific papers and studies on the subject. These studies should all have been shredded on May 6th 1954, when Roger Bannister proved everybody wrong at a race in Oxford. From then on, over a 1000 people have done it.

I highly recommend that you let go of limiting beliefs such as:

- I don't have time
- Whatever I do, I never get my work done
- The more I work, the more work comes up

- I'll never finish this on time

And pick up some empowering beliefs such as:

- I don't know how I do it, but it seems I always find time.
- Every day I get my work done.
- I'm in total control of my work day and always have a reserve of time.
- I'm so productive, I do in 2 hours what my colleagues do in 6.

Here's a little exercise. Ask yourself the following questions:

What do I believe about time? To change a belief, follow this exercise and say to yourself:

1) This is only my belief about reality. That doesn't mean that it is the reality.
2) Although I believe this, it's not necessarily true.
3) Create emotions that are opposite to the belief.
4) Imagine the opposite.
5) Be aware that the belief is only an idea that you have about reality and not reality itself.
6) For just 10 minutes a day, ignore what seems to be real and act as if your wish has come true. (See yourself relaxed, having all the time in the world.)

3

Visualize

Visualization is a fundamental resource in building experiences. The subconscious part of your brain cannot distinguish between a well-done visualization and reality.

This means that if you visualize that you are very productive with a lot of emotion and in great detail, your subconscious mind will be convinced that you really are.

You will then be provided with motivation, opportunities and ideas that will help you to transform yourself into a more productive person.

Does this sound like woo woo to you? Can, for example, sports be practiced by pure visualization?

Well, actually YES. There are various studies that confirm the power of visualization. As early as in the 80s, Tony Robbins worked with the US Army and used visualization techniques to dramatically increase pistol shooting performance.

There have also been other studies for improving free throw shooting percentages of basketball players using the same techniques. The results were amazing! If you look closely at athletes, they all visualize their races and matches.

If it works for the best professional skiers, Formula One drivers, golfers, tennis players and soccer players who visualize in-game situations, days and hours before the actual match, why shouldn't it work for your productivity goals?

Greats like Jack Nicklaus, Wayne Gretzky and Greg Louganis, to name a few, are known to have achieved their goals with visualization.

Thanks to the newest technologies, neuro-scientists have found that the same neurons light up in your brain when you imagine something (for example eating a lemon) as when you are actually doing it!

See yourself as already having achieved the goal of productivity. See it through your own eyes and put all your senses into it: smell it, hear it, feel it, taste it. Can you feel how relaxed you are, now that you have your day under control and enough time for everything that's on your plate?

The more emotions you put into it, the more of an

impact it will have. If you do this for 15 minutes every day, over time you will see enormous results. Make time for you daily visualization, either in your morning ritual or in the evening, before going to bed.

4

Increase Your Energy

To be productive, you need lots of energy. Here's a chapter with lots of recommendations of how to increase you energy and become super productive. It seems like common sense, but once again, **"Common sense is not common action."** You're probably already into most of these habits, but there is nothing like a good reminder.

Surround yourself with the right people

Watch who you are spending your time with. The famous quote "You are the average of the five persons you spend the most time with," once said by Jim Rohn and since then cited in thousands of workshops and books around the world has now been proven to be more than just an empty mantra.

Numerous scientific studies in the field of Positive

Psychology have proven that emotions actually ARE contagious!

It's said that when you put three strangers in a room together, the one who expresses most emotions will transmit his or her mood to the others in just two minutes.

Did you notice that when you feel anxious or are in a negative mood, these feelings affect every interaction you have, whether you want them to or not?

Similarly, you can be affected by overtly negative persons in an instant! Imagine spending lots of time with them. If this can happen in two minutes, imagine what it can do to you in an 8-hour work day or at home!

Luckily, it works the same way with positive emotions. There was an experiment at Yale where while on a group task one member of the group was instructed to be overtly positive. The experiments were videotaped and researchers tracked the emotions of each team member before and after the session. Later the individual and group performances were studied.

Guess what happened…**whenever the positive team member entered the room, his mood instantly infected everybody around him**. More than that, thanks to "happy guy's" positive mood, each individual team member improved their performance and their ability to accomplish their task as a team.

In another experiment, students with bad grades who were rooming with better students improved their grade point averages. Even sports teams can improve their performance having one happy player on their team—and the happier they are, the better they will play!

So you better choose to spend more time with people who bring out the best in you, who motivate you, who believe in you, who empower you instead of people who drag you down.

Stay away from energy vampires. The naysayers, the blamers, the complainers. The people who are always judging or gossiping and talking bad about everything.

People around you can be the springboard to motivate you, help you gain courage and take the right actions, but on the other hand can also drag you down, drain your energy, and act as brakes in the achieving of your life goals and productivity.

Don't spend a lot of time around people who have nothing to do and want to convince you to be like them, mostly to justify their own laziness. ("Let's go for a three-hour lunch, let's finish early today and go for some beer.") Nothing against going out for beer with your friends. Just be on the lookout and analyze if it's for socializing or if you are wasting your time.

If you are around negative people all the time, they can convert you into a negative and cynical person over time. They might want to convince you to stay where you are and keep you stuck, because they value security and don't like risk and uncertainty.

Steve Jobs put it in one short sentence:

"*Don't let the noise of the opinions of others drown your own inner voice.*"

It will be difficult for you to grow and thrive if people around you want to convince you of the contrary.

Unfortunately, oftentimes it's the people closest to you who drag you down, because they want to protect you. So what do you do if it's people close to you? The only thing you can work on is becoming a better, energy-loaded person yourself.

Fortunately, the contagion of emotions works both ways. If you are happy and energy-loaded, you might infuse that spirit in people around you.

If that doesn't work, and you grow and develop, negative people will soon turn away from you because you don't serve their purpose anymore. They need somebody who shares their negativity, and if you don't do that they will look for somebody else.

If all of that doesn't work, you seriously have to ask

yourself if you should start to spend less time with them or stop seeing them altogether. But that's a decision you have to make.

I always distanced myself from people who didn't support me, and I never regretted it, although it wasn't easy!

One of my favourite phrases is, "If your friends and family don't think that you are totally crazy, your goals aren't big enough!"

Here's a little exercise:

Make a list of all the people you have in your life and are spending time with (members of your family, friends, colleagues).

Analyze who is positive for you and who drags you down.

Spend more time with the positive people and stop seeing the toxic people (blamers, complainers) in your life, or at least spend less time with them.

Choose to be around positive people who support you.

Treat your body like a temple

Most of us say that health is the most important thing in our lives; nevertheless many people drink, smoke, eat junk food or even take drugs, and spend most of their free time on the couch without any physical activity. Now, isn't that ironic?

If you adopt some of these little healthy habits into your life, your productivity will probably at least double. Follow a balanced diet, exercise regularly, and stay or get in physical shape so that your brain has all the nutrition it needs to produce a positive lifestyle.

- Eat more fruit and vegetables.
- Reduce your intake of red meat.
- Drink at least two liters of water each day.
- Eat less!
- Stop eating junk food.
- Get up early.

Exercise

We all know it's great, and yet few of us do it. In one mind-boggling study it was proven that exercising three times a week had the same impact on depressed people as taking anti-depressants. But not only that:

the relapse rate among the people that exercised was only 9% compared to over 40% of the study group that took pills.

I guess I'm not coming to you with breaking news here if I tell you how important exercise is for you. The best excuse is always: "I have no time." Funnily enough, if you invest time in exercising, you will improve your productivity and end up having more time.

Here's a list of the benefits that exercising three to five times a week will bring you:

1. It will keep you healthy.
2. It will help you lose weight, which will improve your health and also make you look better.
3. It will make you feel better and you will have a lot of energy.
4. It will improve your self-esteem.
5. You will sleep better.
6. It will reduce stress.

Furthermore, studies show that regular exercise makes you happier, can reduce the symptoms of depression, reduces the risk of disease (heart, diabetes, osteoporosis, high cholesterol, etc.), lowers the risk of a premature death, improves your memory, and helps in many more ways.

Are you in?

One last thing: Don't force yourself to exercise. Enjoy it. Look for a recreational activity that fits you and that you enjoy doing, such as swimming, for example. Even walking an hour a day can make a difference.

Listen to your favorite music

An easy way to feel happy and motivated instantly is to listen to your favorite music! This will boost your productivity instantly. Make a playlist of your all-time favorites and listen to them. Why not make a playlist on your iPod, phone, or PC and listen to them? This will boost your productivity. Give it a try!

I don't know about you, but I work a lot better with music. If I'm writing, I listen to classical or instrumental music and sometimes, while translating, I listen to energy-loaded electronic music of my favorite trance DJs.

Wake up early

The first benefit of getting up an hour earlier is that you gain around 365 hours per year. 365!

Who said "I don't have time"? When clients come

to me telling me that they don't have time, the first thing I ask them is how many hours of TV are they watching. This usually provides them with the time they need.

Those who stop watching TV and still don't have enough time can gain time by getting up an hour earlier.

There is a very special energy in the morning hours before sunrise. My life changed completely ever since I started getting up around 5.30 or 6 A.M.

I usually go for a walk half an hour before the sun rises so that on my way back I see the sun rising "out of" the Mediterranean Sea. This is absolutely fantastic and puts me in a state of absolute happiness. As a consequence, I feel much more clear, focused, calmer and relaxed and don't start the day already running around stressed.

And for those of you who don't live next to the sea: a sunrise "out of" fields, forests or even a big city is just as exciting. Just go watch it and let me know!

Starting your day like this is very beneficial for your happiness and peace of mind. Another great advantage of getting up earlier is that it reinforces self-discipline, and you'll gain self-respect.

All of these benefits will have a tremendous impact on your productivity!

Many successful leaders were, and still are, members of the early birds club: For example, Nelson Mandela, Mahatma Gandhi, Barack Obama, and many more.

It's scientifically proven that 6 hours should be enough sleep per night paired with a 30- to 60-minute power nap in the afternoon.

Your freshness depends on the quality of your sleep, not on the quantity, but you have to try and figure out for yourself how many hours of sleep you need. Give it a try, because once you figure it out, it will improve your quality of life a lot.

Don't forget that getting up early is a new habit, so give it some time and don't give up after the first week if you still feel tired after getting up earlier. The habit needs at least three to four weeks to kick in. If you absolutely can't get up one hour earlier, try half an hour.

And don't forget that your attitude, thoughts and beliefs about getting up an hour earlier play a big role too. To me it was always intriguing how it was so difficult for me to get up at 6.45ish to go to work after 7 or 8 hours of sleep, but before every vacation I usually slept 4 hours and woke up before the alarm clock went off and I was totally refreshed and energized.

In the end, getting up or hitting the snooze button

is a decision you make. It's up to you. How important is a better lifestyle and more time for you?

Read

"The man who doesn't read has no advantage over the man that can't read," says Mark Twain. If you read for half an hour a day that's three and a half hours a week and 182 hours a year! That's a lot of knowledge at your disposal. One of my first written goals during my coaching training was "to read more" (not very specific, but it worked). That was at a time when I hadn't read a book in years.

Now I'm devouring an average of two books a week. I have learnt more in the last two years that in the whole 30 years before including my International Business studies. So always have a book with you. If you substitute the habit of watching TV or, even worse, the news, by reading a good book just before going to bed, you will derive the additional benefit of peace of mind.

Another side effect is that you increase your creativity. So what are you waiting for? Make a list of six books that you will read in the next three months! If you don't know what to read, check out my webpage for recommendations. But make that list NOW!

Take breaks

You might think you don't need breaks and would rather work 10 hours every day to become more productive. Think again! If you deny yourself free time, you'll actually be less productive because when you are tired, you are a lot less efficient. You'll also be less creative and make poorer decisions.

Take a break every now and then and see what it does for you. You will notice that you will be much more productive that way. It's recommended to take a 5-minute break every hour. I usually take half an hour every 2 hours or 2–3 hours after working 4 hours in a row when I'm in a flow state.

Change your posture

This is an exercise taken from Neuro-linguistic Programming which proclaims that changing your posture also changes your mind. People I tell this to usually think that I'm joking. But before writing this off as nonsense...try it out!

When you feel sad and depressed, you usually look

at the floor, your shoulders sag, and adapt the posture of a sad person, right? Now try the following just for a moment: stand upright, shoulders up, chest out, and hold your head up high—you can even exaggerate it by looking up. How does it feel? If you smile, laugh and walk with your head held high, you will realize that you feel a lot better. It's impossible to feel sad walking around like that, isn't it?

And there has been more research conducted on this subject. A study by Brion, Petty and Wagner in 2009 found that people who were sitting straight had higher self-confidence than people sitting slumped over! There is also an amazing TED talk by Amy Cuddy called "Your body language shapes who you are" about the research she did together with Dana Carney at Harvard University. The study has shown that holding "power postures" for 2 minutes creates a 20% increase in testosterone (which boosts confidence) and a 25% decrease in cortisol (which reduces stress). Imagine this. If you have an important presentation, reunion or competition, just take on the posture of a confident person for two minutes. Put your hands on your hips and spread your feet (think Wonder Woman) or lean back in a chair and spread your arms. Hold the posture for at least two minutes...and see what happens!

Try and watch Amy Cuddy's TED talk "Your body language shapes who you are".

It does miracles for me before presentations, or being on radio or TV.

5

Celebrate Your Wins!

"Celebrate what you want to see more of," says Thomas Peters. On your way forward to more productivity and reaching your goals, it's also important to be aware of your progress!

Stop every now and then and celebrate your wins! Celebrate that you have come further than you were last week. Celebrate that you have crossed a lot of things off of that to-do list of yours. Celebrate that you don't pick up your phone on Tuesdays for two hours and work super focused during that time.

If you want to write a book, celebrate for every 2000 words you have written.

Don't let your small victories go unnoticed! This will help you stay motivated.

Every action step completed is worth celebrating.

It doesn't have to be big stuff. You can celebrate with a walk among nature or take a morning off and go to a museum. Or a night at the movies alone or with your sweetheart. Be creative. But celebrate!

6
Take Control

It's scientifically proven that you'll be more successful and therefore more productive if you adopt the belief that you have control over your life. If you are a student you will be happier, get better grades, and more motivation to pursue a career you really want; if you are an employee, feeling in control will have you do a better job and be more satisfied with it.

There is only one person who's responsible for your life and that is YOU! You are the designer of your life and of your productivity. Not your boss, not your spouse, not your parents, not your friends, not your clients, not the economy, not the weather. YOU!

If you don't have time in your life, you are making the wrong decisions. It's not THEM who call you whenever they feel like it, **it's YOU taking the call**.

It's not THEM always giving you extra work, **it's YOU being too afraid to put your foot down** and say,

"I'm sorry I can't take on this task."

It's not THEM who distract you from work, **it's YOU letting them distract you**.

The day your stop blaming others for everything that happens in your life, everything changes!

Taking responsibility for your life is taking charge of your life and becoming the protagonist of it. It's one of the most liberating experiences you can have.

Science has proven that believing you are in control leads to success in nearly every aspect of your life, and not just at work. You'll be much happier, will have less stress at work, and be more motivated, which is the perfect formula to boost your productivity.

The fun thing is that psychologists found out that to reap all these benefits it doesn't even matter a lot if you **really** have that control; it's more important that you think you have it. That's no surprise keeping in mind how your beliefs, expectations and attitudes shape your experience of the world.

Instead of being a victim of your circumstances, you obtain the power to create your own circumstances or at least the power to decide how you are going to act in the face of circumstances that life presents to you.

It doesn't matter what happens to you in your life; it matters what attitude you adopt towards what happens to you. And the attitude you adopt is your choice!

If you blame others for not having enough time, what has to happen to make you find more time? All of the others have to change! And that, my friend, I tell you, is not going to happen.

If you are the protagonist, YOU have the power to change the things that you don't like in your life! You are in control of your thoughts, actions and feelings. You are in control of your time and the people you spend your time with.

If you don't like your results, change your input—your thoughts, emotions and expectations. Stop reacting to others and start responding. Reaction is automatic. Responding is consciously choosing your response.

You don't depend on external factors. Life happens, but you choose your behavior. The solutions of your problems are not on the outside—thanks to options and the power of choice. Your success only depends on you. The sooner you can embrace this, the better it gets.

Yes. Bad things happen to good people. You can still choose to make the best out of the circumstances.

Act where you have control and accept where you don't have control, and above all, don't lose your time on subjects that are out of your control.

The victim says, "Every bad thing in my life is other

people's fault", but if you are not part of the problem, then you also can't be a part of the solution or—in other words—if the problem is caused by the outside, the solution is also on the outside.

So, once again, even if you don't have control over the stimuli that the environment sends you continuously, you have the liberty to **choose** your behavior, of how you will face the situation.

The person with a "victim mentality" only reacts, is always innocent, and constantly blames others for his or her life situation while using the past as justification and putting their hopes on a future which will miraculously bring solutions to problems or a change in others who are causing the trouble. This is pretty risky and probably neither one nor the other is going to happen.

Protagonists know that they are responsible, choose adequate behavior, and hold themselves accountable. They use the past as a valuable experience from which to learn, live in the present where they see constant opportunities for change, and decide and go after their future goals.

The most important question is: **"Who will you choose to be—by your actions—when life presents you with these circumstances?"**

Choices and decisions

Your life is the result of the decisions you made. How do you feel about that? Is this true for you? It's important that from now on, you are aware of the power you have over your life by making decisions!

Every decision, every choice has an important influence on your life. In fact, your life is a direct result of the choices and decisions you made in the past, and every choice carries a consequence!

The most important thing is to make decisions. Whether the decision is right or wrong is secondary. You will soon receive feedback that will help you to progress. Once you have made a decision, go with it and accept the consequences. If it was wrong, learn from it and forgive yourself, knowing that at that point in time, and with the knowledge you had, it was the best and the right decision to take.

YOUR ATTITUDE + YOUR DECISIONS = YOUR LIFE

Viktor Frankl was a Jewish psychologist imprisoned in concentration camps during the Second World War. He lost his entire family except his sister. Under these terrible circumstances, he became aware of what he named "the ultimate human freedom", which not even the Nazi prison wards could take away from him: they could control his external circumstances, but in the last instance, it was him who CHOSE HOW these circumstances were going to affect him!

He found out that between STIMULUS and RESPONSE there was a small space in time in which he had the freedom to CHOOSE his RESPONSE! This means that even if you may not be able to control the circumstances that life presents to you, you can always choose your response in facing those circumstances, and by doing so, have a huge impact on your life.

In other words, what hurts us is not what happens to us, but our response to what happens to us. The most important thing is how we RESPOND to what happens to us in our lives. And that is a CHOICE!

Do you want to have more time? Make better choices about who you surround yourself with, how you plan your work, how many favors you do for others, which phone calls you take, and so on. You now have the knowledge you need to become a productivity machine and find lots of time. The decision to apply this knowledge is yours to take. There are no excuses!

7
Smile More

Smile! Even if you don't feel like it! Smiling improves the quality of your life, health and relationships...and your productivity! It's proven that every little shot of happiness improves your work performance and productivity.

If you don't do it already, start to smile consciously today. It's confirmed that laughing and smiling is extremely good for your health!

Science has demonstrated that laughing or smiling a lot daily improves your mental state and your creativity. So laugh more!

Make it a point to watch at least an hour of comedy or fun stuff a day and laugh until tears roll down your cheeks! You will feel a lot better and full of energy once you get into this habit. Give it a try!

Tara Kraft and Sarah Pressman at the University of Kansas demonstrated that smiling can alter your stress response in difficult situations.

The study showed that it can slow your heart rate down and decrease stress levels—even if you are not feeling happy.

It's proven that not only do your emotions influence you physiology, but also the other way round. Smiling sends a signal to your brain that things are all right.

Just try it next time you feel stressed or overwhelmed, and let me know if it works. If you think you have no reason at all to smile, hold a pen or a chopstick with your teeth.

It simulates a smile and might produce the same effects.

If you need even more incentives for smiling, search for the study by Wayne University on smiling which has found a link between smiling and longevity!

When you smile, your entire body sends out the message "Life is great" to the world. Studies show that smiling people are perceived as more confident and more likely to be trusted. People just feel good around them.

Further benefits of smiling are:

- Releases serotonin (makes us feel good)
- Releases endorphins (lowers pain)
- Lowers blood pressure

- Increases clarity
- Boosts the functioning of your immune system
- Provides a more positive outlook towards life (Try being a pessimist while you smile…)

8
Fake It Till You Become It!

There is a lot of truth in William James' words, "If you want a quality, act as if you already have it."

Act as if! Act as if you already are productive. Act as if you already have the quality of life, the lifestyle, the job that a productive person has.

If you want to be more productive, you have to start acting as if you already are.

Speak like a productive person, walk like a productive person, have the body posture of a productive person.

Your subconscious cannot differentiate between reality and imagination. Use this to your advantage by acting "as if" you already have the strength, the character trait, etc. In Neuro-linguistic Programming and coaching, this is called modeling.

A good way to become successful and productive is to observe and copy already successful and productive people. If they have made it, you can do it too. If you look very closely, the most successful persons are oftentimes also the most productive ones.

This works! It's actually what I did. I became productive using all the tricks successful and productive people explained in their books and talks. And look at me: six, seven years ago, I was not productive and not organized at all, and today I'm writing a book about productivity…

Start acting "as if" and see what happens. Fake it till you make it!

9

Your Attitude

Your attitude is crucial for everything including your time management!

It can change your way of seeing things dramatically and also your way of facing them. You will suffer less in life and at your workplace if you accept the rules of the game. Life is made up of laughter and tears, light and shadow. You have to accept the bad moments by changing your way of looking at them. Everything that happens to you is a challenge and an opportunity at the same time.

Always look at the positive side of things in life, even in the worst situations. Sometimes it might take some time to discover it, but there is something good hidden in every bad. Take a moment and look back. Isn't it true? Your partner left you and you were destroyed, but today you are happier than ever with your new love. A business deal went sour, but today you are happy it did, because an even better opportunity came up…

Remember: It's not what happens in your life that's important; it's how you respond to what happens to you that makes your life!

Life is a chain of moments—some happy, some sad—and it depends on YOU to make the best of each and every one of those moments.

Many years ago all of the success teachers and positive thinkers described it this way:

"If life gives you a lemon, add sugar to it, and make lemonade out of it." Younger readers might say that "If life gives you a lemon, ask for some salt and tequila." You get the point, don't you?

So, allow yourself to make mistakes and learn from them. Admit that there are things you don't know. Dare asking for help and let other people surprise you with the help they offer you.

Differentiate between what you have done in your life until now and what you want to do—or better still—will do from now on!

Now go out and get your life back. You can do it, and above all—you've earned it!

10
Watch Your Words

"The only thing that's keeping you from getting what you want is the story you keep telling yourself."

—TONY ROBBINS

Watch your words! Don't underestimate them! They are very powerful! The words that we use to describe our experiences become our experiences. You probably encountered a situation or two in your life when spoken words did a lot of damage. And this is true not only in talking to others, but also in talking to yourself. Yes, this little voice in your head— the one that just asked, "Voice, what voice?"

Words can affect your performance, and also the performance and mindsets of others. Remember the Pygmalion Effect? What you expect from yourself and/ or other people is transmitted by your words, and your words have a very powerful effect, not only on your results, but also on the results of your friends, colleagues or family.

You are what you tell yourself the whole day! Your inner dialogue is like the repeated suggestion of a hypnotist. Are you complaining a lot about not having time? What story are you telling yourself?

If you run around telling yourself that you never have time, I'm afraid that's what you will find in your world.

On the other hand, if you say you always find time and are a super productive person, you will reflect that, and the outer environment will fall into place. Of course, talking, alone, is not enough. You have to take action and apply some of the time management tricks you have learnt by now.

Your inner dialogue has a huge impact on your self-esteem. So be careful with how you describe yourself: such as "I'm lazy", "I'm a disaster", "I'll never be able to do that", "I just don't get things done on time", or my personal favourite "I'm tired" because, of course, the more you tell yourself that you are tired, the more tired you will get!

Watching your inner dialogue is very important! The way you communicate with yourself changes the way you think about yourself, which changes the way you feel about yourself, which changes the way you act, and this ultimately influences your results and the perception that others have of you.

Keep the conversation with yourself positive such as "I want to achieve great productivity", "I want to have a lot of free time" and "God, I am good", because your subconscious mind doesn't understand the little word "NO". It sees your words as IMAGES.

Don't think of a pink elephant! See? I bet you just imagined a pink elephant.

And—I will repeat myself—please focus on what you want. Keep in mind that your words, and especially the questions you ask yourself, have a huge influence on your reality. I tell my coaching clients to never tell me or themselves that they have no time, but instead always ask, "How can I find more time?" or "How can I get more done?"

If you ask yourself "how", your brain will search for an answer and come up with it. The good thing is that you can really change your life by changing your language, talking to yourself in a positive way, and starting to ask yourself different questions.

Why wait? Start asking yourself different questions now!

The two powerful words "What if?"

> *"Our expectancies not only affect how we see reality but also affect the reality itself."*

—DR EDWARD E. JONES

Always expect the best! Life doesn't always give you what you want, but it sure gives you what you expect! Do you expect success? Or do you spend most of your time worrying about failure? Your expectations about yourself and others come from your subconscious beliefs, and they have an enormous impact on your achievements.

Your expectations influence your attitude and your attitude has a lot to do with your productivity. They also affect your willingness to take action, and all of your interactions with others.

Many of us know all this and yet, most of us expect negative outcomes when asking one of the favorite questions of the mind: The question "What if".

By asking it, we are often focused on what doesn't work: "What if it doesn't work out?", "What if the stuff Marc writes about doesn't work?", "What if I don't get the job done?", "What if I never find time?"

However, neither does this feel good, nor is it good

to focus on what we fear. Why not turn this around and ask yourself for every limiting or negative thought, **"What if the opposite is true?"**, "What if this works out great?", "What if this little book changes my life?", "What if this stuff works?", "What if I finish this project on time?" or "What if I finally find time?"

The single adjustment in how you ask your questions transforms you, your energy, and the answer you get. It changes your thinking and your inner dialogue.

Suddenly you start asking positive "What if" questions in your head, rather than negative ones. The benefits of changing your thinking will mean:

- You will go through less stress, fear, and anxiety.
- You will feel more peaceful.
- Your energy levels will go up.
- It allows you to be the inventor of your own experience.

Try it out! How did you feel just now reading it? Write a list of all of your fears and negative "What if"s and then turn them around.

IV

RECAP

1

Burning Out

Burnout creeps into your life silently. Watch very closely if you notice the following symptoms:

- You work more and more hours and get less and less done.
- You don't sleep very well any more.
- You start hating what you do and questioning yourself if it's all worth it.
- You sit in front of your computer the whole day and notice at the end of the day that you got nothing done.
- What normally took you hours now takes days.

There is such a thin line between working a lot on your business or career being motivated to do it all and slowly burning out that you don't even notice it at first. When you notice it you just drag yourself from day to day and have already lost the joy of working on your business or at your job till you might be at the point of crossing that line.

Ask yourself the following questions:

1. Have you lost your enthusiasm?
2. Do you get much less done now than before?
3. Did you run out of ideas and momentum?
4. Is it difficult for you to get up in the morning and get to work—or do you even hate it?

If you answer one or more of those questions with a YES, then you might want to have a look at whether your are burning out.

Many people think that in order to build their business or their career they have to work 20 hours a day and can't take a day or a weekend off. There's some truth to it, but unfortunately it's the fast lane to burnout.

As we have learnt now, taking breaks every now and then and on weekends will not damage your productivity. It will actually boost it!

Don't work 60 hours a week thinking that once you are successful you can cut down your hours. Start cutting down your hours and take breaks to become successful quicker.

I bet that most of my readers can cut their hours in half. Use as many tricks as you can from this book. Of course you have to work a lot, but being productive, you might not have to put that many hours in, just make the most of the hours (remember Pareto and company).

There is a huge different between putting in hours and wasting them.

Taking short breaks every now and then revitalizes you and you'll get a lot more work done afterwards. You will also become more creative, get new ideas, be happier, and therefore be better in coping with obstacles in your way. I'd even go as far as to say that not taking time off is wasting working time!

When you notice that you are not getting as much done as you should, forgetting things, or feeling like you are simply staring at your computer screen for hours without getting anything done, it's time to take a break.

How to prevent burning out:

1. **Take time off every week**. At least one day.
2. **Get enough sleep**. Most of the time it's better to go to bed before midnight and get up early the next day. If you work until 2 A.M. in the morning you are usually less productive the next day. However,

this also depends on your rhythm. If you are a night owl it might just work out great for you. That's something you have to try out for yourself. Lack of sleep will definitely accelerate burning out.

3. **Take good care of yourself**. Read a good book, go to the movies, get a massage, watch a sunrise, sit by the water, go for a walk, take a bubble bath, etc. Treating yourself well will do miracles for your productivity with the positive side effect of lifting your self-confidence and self-esteem!

4. **Ditch projects**. Remember Pareto? Find out which 20% of your projects are bringing IN 80% of the money and ditch the rest. Ditch the projects that are very time intensive, demand too much effort, and bring in relatively less money. Be selective about what new projects you accept. There's nothing better than a project that you don't really want. Double the price. If you still get the project, outsource most of it.

2
Tools Put into Practice

Managing your time

- Invest a few hours in defining exactly what you want to do
- Plan—take 15 minutes the day before or 15 minutes before you start your day to plan it out
- Prioritize
- Do the uncomfortable first (Brian Tracy would say "Eat that frog")
- Block time and learn to say "No"
- Group similar tasks ("Batch")
- Use a task list
- Keep an Interruptions log
- Keep track of your time for at least a week

Conflicts

- Listen with the intention of understanding—not with the intention to answer
- Negotiate "win-win situations"
- Go for collaboration rather than confrontation
- Be willing to take the first step
- Explain what you need and why and let the other person know how they can help
- Take a deep breath
- Remember—"We see the world not as it is but as we are"

Organize your email

- Set aside the time needed for a "BIG" inbox organization
- Organize or create files according to your needs
- Move all emails that are older than a month to a "temporary file" (if you haven't touched them in six months…delete them)
- Divide the project into smaller tasks—work on your emails an hour every day.
- Commit to go home with a clean mailbox every evening.
- Remember: Do it now, file it for later, delegate it,

file for reference, delete.

- The more you postpone this task, the uglier it gets.
- Handle emails that come from other parts of the world first thing in the morning.
- Educate your team to copy you only on emails that are really important.
- Use Skype (or similar) to handle things that are typically distributed in several emails.
- Assign at least one morning or afternoon in a week to work without interruptions.

Work fast

- Set goals and allocate time for each one.
- Commit to keep given times.
- Avoid distractions.
- Group similar tasks (batching).
- Block time for your tasks,; do not allow interruptions.
- Learn to say "NO".
- Focus on your goals, visualize results, prioritize.
- Remember the Pareto principle: 20% of your effort will give you 80% of your results.

Too much work?

- Define priorities—remember the time management matrix.
- Allocate time for your most important tasks and stick to it.
- Check if all you have to do is really necessary. Can you delegate? Automate?
- Do you need to talk to your boss about your workload?

When you are relying on others

- Write down what you need from the other person.
- Write how the person impacts your delay.
- Think in advance about how you might reach a solution. Present alternatives.
- Use positive language.
- Have a meeting or private call with the person.
- Be honest, polite and understanding.
- If the person ignores your request, talk to your boss.

How to deal with interruptions

- Learn to say "NO" in a friendly manner and schedule time for later.

- Inform people that you will be grateful if from now on your time "without interruption" is respected.
- Use headphones.
- Go to a place where you cannot be interrupted.
- Let calls go to voicemail.
- Negotiate with a coworker to be able to redirect the call when you're busy.
- Analyze if it's really necessary to attend all the meetings you are invited to.
- Help others, but do not make it a permanent habit.

Everything is urgent

- Prioritize and check the importance of each task.
- If you get to the point where everything is urgent, your workload must be revised.
- Analyze why all of your tasks are urgent. Are you procrastinating? Are you organized? Are your coworkers organized? Are there any technical problems?
- Avoid jumping between tasks.
- Explain in a calm voice that you are ending task # 1, and when it's done you will go to task # 2…Explain politely WHEN your task will be completed. People do not want to hear that you're busy; they just want to know when you'll be done with their stuff.

Managing distractions

- Make a list of things you have to do during the day.
- Prioritize.
- Commit to finishing your tasks before the day is over.
- Reward yourself for finished tasks.
- Ask a colleague to help you achieve your goal of the day.
- Disconnect your phone.
- Disconnect everything that distracts you. Work without distractions for at least one hour a day.

Inconsistency and lack of commitment in the implementation

- One small step every day—if you fail, do not beat yourself up. Try again the next day.
- Remember, no one else will do it for you.
- Do the most uncomfortable task first thing in the morning each day for a week and check results.
- Reward yourself.
- Use the tools that are easy for you (list, group tasks, etc.).

Multitasking

- Avoid it—many studies show that multitasking is less productive.
- Use the time management matrix and do one thing at a time.
- You need discipline: avoid looking at your emails constantly; don't answer messages/private calls; don't get distracted into doing things that are not important.
- Plan your day in "time blocks" that you will devote to specific tasks and follow through.
- Every time you have completed a task, take a break and then go to the next one.

Loud environment

- Use ear plugs/headphones.
- Change your work space to a quieter space.
- Do important things very early in the morning, at noon, or at night.
- If things get really bad, take a walk to "gather your thoughts".

Afraid to make mistakes

- We are all in a constant learning process, therefore, ask for help! Your boss will appreciate it.
- Remember: It's better to be nervous once than regretting it later.
- If the worst happens…think philosophically: we learn more from our mistakes.
- Talk to your boss and explain what areas need help (training, mentoring, coaching, etc.).

Difficulties in follow-up/forgetting the customers' problems

- Use an electronic calendar.
- Schedule the follow-up the same way you'd program a meeting or any other task.
- Set a phone alarm.
- Write down the "problem" as a task and be sure to follow up.

Too curious to not check incoming emails

- Turn off notifications for incoming emails.
- Assign specific times during the day for accessing your email.

- Commit to not check emails all the time. Nobody can make you do what you do not want to do.
- Reward yourself when you refrain from taking a look at the inbox.
- Keep track of the time you spend going back and forth to look at your emails and compare it with the time you spend when you focus on your tasks and agree to check emails only a few times per day.

Too many meetings

- Evaluate whether you really have to attend all meetings.
- If you attend, do you have to stay for the entire meeting?
- Try to schedule days without meetings where you can concentrate on your other tasks.
- Delegate attending meetings or other tasks.

3

One Last Thing...

I want you to have all the time wasters in one chapter. This is a little summary of the most "dangerous" time robbers and how to manage them, and I added this section to make sure you really get your productivity to the next level. If you manage these time drains effectively, they won't harm your productivity.

Email

Turning off email notifications will boost your productivity (remember that every beep or vibration is a distraction that costs you between 7 and 25 minutes).

More tricks

- Set yourself a fixed time during the day and set a time limit for checking your emails. For example, three times a day for half an hour, in the morning, afternoon and evening.

- For emails that you need longer to respond to, send the person a quick message like: "I received your message and will send you a detailed reply later." Add this to your task list.
- Organize your email inbox.
- Have different accounts for you personal and work emails so that personal emails don't distract you.
- Create an "away" message that tells the sender that you received their email and that you'll get back to them as soon as possible.
- Create email templates for similar emails that you send.

The internet

Oftentimes you go online to research some information and before your know it it's lunch time and you have been looking at random YouTube videos for the last two hours. It's very easy to get lost in the endless space of the internet.

- The best solution is to stay away from the web! If you have to go online anyway, keep your goal in mind! What specific bit of information are you looking for? Which task are you looking to accomplish?

- Log out of your social media accounts. Period.
- Turn off notifications from social media apps on your phone.
- Use free time or down time for your social media. For example, waiting in line at the supermarket while responding to messages via your mobile device. I usually do my social media on the train to Barcelona. If you use social media for your job, schedule time for it, stay on task when using it, and stay away from it when it's not scheduled.

Phone calls

Not all phone calls are important and you don't have to receive calls all the time. Every now and then you may have no choice but to answer the phone, though.

- Maximize productivity by keeping your calls short and focused on important business.
- Let the call go to your voice mail and let people know when they can expect a reply.
- Schedule a time to call the person back later.
- Redirect the incoming phone calls to a colleague for a determined time. The colleague can inform

the caller when it is okay to call you. Do the same for your colleague so that they can also become more productive.

Meetings

My personal opinion: Skip 'em or don't have 'em. (I'm clearly damaged by unproductive meetings.) If that's not possible, keep meetings to a minimum and keep them as short as possible.

- Have a clear starting and ending time.
- Let everybody know what the goal of the meeting is.
- Stay focused on the important stuff and let people know what they need to do before attending the meeting.
- Hold standing or walking meetings. They usually end quicker.
- Use Google Hangouts or Skype if possible instead of meeting in person.

Colleagues

There are several ways to handle coworkers if they present a distraction.

- Isolate yourself physically. Close your door. Use headphones (like me—writing this chapter on the train again...).
- Say "No" to requests until you have your tasks under control.
- Tell people when you are busy and when they can interrupt you.
- Offer them help at a later time.

Mundane tasks

There are some tasks that just have to be done. Here are four ways to get rid of them:

1. Eliminate
2. Delegate
3. Outsource
4. Automate

And by all means don't run any errands for your colleagues, family and friends. If you are the one running the errands for everybody, you will never find time. Period. Running errands for others is a huge time waster, and if you are the good guy that does many favors, everybody will like you, but you will never have time, and if you are an entrepreneur you'll probably go bankrupt. So watch closely which errands you run and for whom. *(If you run errands for everybody and still are successful and have all the time in the world, please let me know. I have never met anybody like you!)*

Mindless entertainment

While examining my clients' time, I found that often they are losing a lot of time on mindless entertainment: TV, video games, social media, YouTube videos, online games, etc.

On one hand it's important to take your mind off your work every now and then and distract yourself a little. The problem starts when you lose control of it or when you just cannot differentiate anymore between relaxing time and work time.

Set clear rules and time for work and fun. When you work you work and when you play you play.

Conclusion

This is it! I hope you had fun and that you now have a lot of tools and habits that can help you increase your productivity and thus help you get more done, have more time for your family, more free time in general, or more time to make money.

Whatever you decide, the choice is yours. There are no more excuses. You now know that "I don't have time for you", most of the time means "You are not important enough for me".Remember you don't have to do it all. You can start with one or two habits from this book and you don't even have to do big things. As you saw from the example of Steve, the stressed sales manager, just changing small things on a daily basis can gain you enormous amounts of time.

The important thing as always is **doing it!** Remember that small steps constantly taken can bring huge results. Don't wait for the future to solve your time management problems magically. Take control. Start **NOW** and I assure you in one year you'll be grateful you started today.

For starters, work the basics such as planning, scheduling, prioritizing. Adopt two or three productivity habits and be very aware of the inner game of productivity. You've got this!

Please let me know what you think about this book. As you saw at the beginning, I really take your feedback seriously. Constructive critics are always welcome and will help me to improve future books or even future editions of this one.

Get in touch with me over Facebook, Twitter, or send me an email at marc@marcreklau.com. I like to be in touch with my readers. :-)

It would be great if you could take the time to leave an honest review on Amazon. This helps other people find the book and if it's five stars…even better ;-)

All the best, and I wish you lots of time!

Acknowledgments

First of all, thanks to my family—who still can't believe what is actually happening since the breakthrough of *30 Days—Change Your Habits, Change Your Life: A Couple of Simple Steps Every Day to Create the Life You Want*, and to my friends who have been there always.

Thank you to the fabulous new people that have entered my life in the last 12 months since starting this adventure and also to those who have left and are on different paths now.

And last but not least, thank YOU, dear reader. Thank you for picking up a copy of this book or for downloading it on Amazon and thank you for taking your valuable time to read it.

Hopefully when you are finished you will have found more time in your life than you could ever imagine.

Printed in Poland
by Amazon Fulfillment
Poland Sp. z o.o., Wrocław